The Princess Imposter

The Princess Imposter

By Vivian Vande Velde

Scholastic Inc.

ISBN 978-1-338-22815-1

10 9 8 7 6 5 4 3 2 1   18 19 20 21 22

Printed in China   68

First printing 2018

Book design by Baily Crawford and Maeve Norton

To the vets and vet techs
who—like Phleg and her
family—look after animals.

table of contents

Perfect

Once upon a time there was a princess named Gabriella, who was beautiful and sweet-natured and much beloved by her family (all of whom were in good health) and by all the people of the kingdom (which was at peace with all their neighboring kingdoms and which was situated in a region of the world not plagued by dragons or ogres or naming-day curses), and she was betrothed to a perfectly nice prince of whom everyone approved and with whom she was certain she would fall madly in love in the next year or so when she would be old enough for such things.

In short, Princess Gabriella had a perfect life.

—Until a band of misbehaving fairies kidnapped her and substituted one of their own in her place.

Chapter 1

Welcome to a New World!

PRINCESS GABRIELLA

Princess Gabriella opened her eyes and saw that she was surrounded by about a dozen fairy children, all crouched around where she lay. *Definitely* not in her own bed, she recognized with a certain amount of alarm, which she didn't allow to show. Nor even in her room. Nor—she had a sinking feeling—anyplace else in her father's kingdom.

The children were staring and giggling. By the tenderness in her side, she suspected they had been poking her. Princesses are not generally accustomed to being stared at or giggled at. Certainly not poked at.

Still, despite her original impression that they must have been jabbing at her with pointed sticks, she saw that none of the children held any implements. It was simply that—being of a slighter build than humans—fairies have fingers that seem sharper, just the way a pin seems sharper than a nail.

Though alarmed by her unexpected situation, Gabriella knew that it was not good to show fear. This is especially true for

2

royalty. In addition, she was gracious and considerate, both by nature and by training, so she decided it would be rude to scream or to weep or to complain or to mention she thought fairies had bony fingers.

She didn't sit up, not yet. Partly this was because taking the time to observe was better done sooner rather than later. But there was another reason she didn't get up: All she was wearing was a nightgown, which—though it covered her adequately—was under no circumstances proper public attire for a princess.

The children wore clothing that brought wildflowers to Gabriella's mind, not only because of the bright colors but even more so because the shapes of the garments suggested blossoms and petals.

Some of the fairies were boys, some girls, some . . . well, with some of them, Gabriella couldn't be sure. The youngest was a toddler with a low-hanging diaper—the source of at least some of the bad smell that the princess had to use all her will-power to pretend not to notice. The eldest was a boy Gabriella judged to be a year or two older than she, though she estimated that if they were standing next to each other, his head would come only to her shoulder.

Another way she could tell immediately that they were fairies was because of the delicate though pinched features of their faces, the slight shimmer of their skin, and the fact that they all had silver-white hair—except for the toddler, who had no hair at all.

Well, and the wings. They had iridescent wings much like those of dragonflies. She had never met a fairy before, but she knew from her bestiary studies that despite their beauty, fairy wings are, aerodynamically speaking, as almost-useless as those of chickens.

All that taken in, Gabriella deemed that *now* was the time to start the process of arising. So she sat up, which caused most of the fairies to scramble to their feet and step back. Except for the toddler, who'd been standing all along and now swayed and grabbed a fistful of material from the skirt of Gabriella's night-dress to keep his or her balance. And the oldest boy, who grinned impertinently at her.

At home, Gabriella's own bed had a mattress made of the finest goose down, and there were satin sheets delicately scented with lavender, and every night a servant would set a cup of honey-flavored milk on her nightstand. Here, Gabriella saw she'd been laid onto one of several piles of straw strewn on the floor. And the straw did not smell much better than that diaper. She was too well-brought-up to scratch at the itch on her arm (princesses are too refined to have itches), but she did glance down and notice a spider making its way across her skin.

Serenity, she reminded herself. In theory, she appreciated all God's creations, but in practice found it hard to warm up to crea-tures in excess of four legs. Still, few onlookers could have sus-pected this, as she calmly observed, "What a fine specimen," and blew gently so that the creature landed, unharmed and fully upright, back down on the straw from which it had no doubt come.

"Hello," she said quietly, so as not to startle the children, because that would have been bad manners, no matter what was going on. "Who are you?"

4

Immediately the children started imitating her, as though they found her formal manner of speaking amusing. "Hello. Hello," they said in snooty tones, bending themselves in two as they bowed to one another—boys, girls, and indeterminates alike.

The oldest one snorted. "Really? That's what you wanna ask? That's your most pressing question? You're looking for courtly introductions?"

The smaller ones continued bowing and began adding phrases to their repertoire, things like "La-dee-da" and "To whom do I have the pleasure of speaking?"

Gabriella smiled indulgently. "Do I only *have* one question?" she asked.

"Iffen you did," the boy told her, "you'd've gone and wasted it. Twice now."

"All right," Gabriella said, grateful for all the lessons she'd had in patience and deportment. "Then how about this one: Where am I?"

"You're here with us," the boy said, making needlessly complicated hand gestures, somewhat like a magician in the town square showing he has nothing up his sleeves, "while our sister Phleg's gone and changed places with you."

"Changeling! Changeling!" the younger ones chorused, now running in circles around one another and occasionally using their wings to lift high enough to avoid collisions.

Of course she was troubled. And yet she knew that in the normal tradition of changelings, fairies sometimes exchanged one of their fussy, colicky babies for a happy, well-behaved human baby. They'd cast a spell to make the fairy babe look like the human one, so that the family would not grow suspicious—assuming, of course, no one noticed the total personality transformation. Once the fairy brat outgrew its foul disposition, its fairy parents would generally trade back.

Gabriella had never heard of someone as old as she was being substituted, and this was worrisome.

And if there was a fairy magically transformed to look like her, did that mean that *she* . . .

Discreetly, Gabriella pulled a strand of her hair forward. She was relieved to see it was the same brown color it had always been. At least she'd been left with her own appearance.

Even with all these thoughts racing through her head—and despite the children mocking the idea of introductions—she couldn't ignore her training in proper protocol. "Your sister *who?*" Gabriella asked. "Flag?" She held her hand out to the boy, a gentle reminder—since he seemed to have forgotten his manners—of his duty to offer her his assistance.

"Phleg," the boy repeated, not seeming to notice her extended hand. He rolled his eyes in exasperation. "Just like *phlegm*, only you pronounce the *g* instead of the *m*."

Gabriella, who was perfectly capable of standing on her own, did so. "Excuse me?"

The boy obviously mistook her incredulity for lack of familiarity with the word. "Phlegm," he repeated. He also stood, proving that Gabriella's estimate of his height—or lack thereof—was accurate. Then he gave a great snorting cough and hacked up a wad of something mucusy, which he spat out on the floor by her feet.

6

"Why?" Gabriella asked. "Why would you do such a thing?" The question could have covered any one of several of her concerns, but the boy only shrugged and answered, "We was bored. Seemed like a good idea at the time."

"How lovely," Gabriella said, recovering her decorum. "I'm sure it will be a learning experience for both . . . Phleg . . . and myself. I am Princess Gabriella of Fairhaven, daughter of King Humphrey and—"

The boy shrugged. "You're Phleg while you're here. And she's you while she's there."

"Indeed," Gabriella murmured, not wanting to argue. "And who are you?"

"Parf."

"*Parf*," Gabriella repeated.

"It's *barf*, but with pee." He slapped his knees and hooted with laughter. "Get it? Get it? Barf with pee." He sighed. "You don't get it."

And she hadn't, not for the first few moments, and once she did, she estimated the politest thing was to continue to pretend she didn't. *You awful, awful fairy boy*, she thought. But as soon as she did, she felt guilty for her unkind thought.

She resolved to be a better person from now on.

PHLEG

Phleg spread her arms and legs out, reaching for all four corners of the bed. *Oooh, nice*, she thought. *I could get used to this.*

It was such a pleasure to not have to share a bed with her half-dozen-or-so younger sisters, who squirmed, and chattered, and sometimes leaked. It was so nice not to have to share a room with her half-dozen-or-so brothers, who whined, and sniveled, and liked nothing better than to pick fights with one another or the sisters or herself. There was nothing in the world, Phleg thought, worse than a younger brother—except, of course, for an older brother.

She rolled around on the cool, smooth satin sheets, wondering if this was how a pig in the mud felt. Until she slid right out from between the slippery things and landed on the floor. *Ow!* she thought, rubbing her head where she had bumped it against the stupid table that some stupid person had stupidly put right by the stupid bed.

But then she thought she was the one being stupid. How could anyone know she had been grievously injured if she only *thought* it?

"Ow!" she howled. "Ow! Ow! Owwwwww!" Not that she was expecting sympathy. She never got sympathy at home. But if she was hurting or unhappy, she preferred to share the misery.

Immediately, someone from the other side of the door knocked knuckles against the wood. "Princess Gabriella? What's amiss? I'm coming in."

Of course, Phleg had cast the spell that made her look like the princess even before she'd done the spell to transport the princess *out* and herself *in*. The servant who came into the room clearly never suspected anything.

Then again, Phleg quickly decided that the servant wasn't very bright. "Oh my!" the woman said, "Princess Gabriella! Are you hurt?"

"No," Phleg told her. "I always like to huddle on the floor going *Ow!* while my brains dribble out of the craterlike wound in my head."

"Oh," the woman said. "Have you hurt your head?"

"Well, duh!" Phleg said, and she held her hand out to show the brain matter that coated it. But surely . . . she didn't know that much about people . . . but didn't people have red blood? Phleg licked the sticky white substance that coated her fingers from where she had touched what she assumed was the gash on her head. Milk.

Meanwhile, the servant had rushed over and used her apron to dab at Phleg's head. "There's a bump . . . ," she said doubtfully, clearly unimpressed by the enormity of the injury.

"Well, then, stop making such a fuss," Phleg ordered her, "and move out of my way so I can stand." What kind of mush-for-brains put a cup of milk right by someone's bed, where it could easily tip over on top of someone who happened to fall out of that bed? And what was a bed doing so high up off the ground in any case?

Phleg surged to her feet as gracefully as a walrus, missing the lift her wings would have given her.

The servant woman put out an arm, which Phleg suspiciously swatted away, as she had fallen once too often for her brothers' pretenses of helping.

"You're certain you're all recovered now?" the servant asked. "You seem a bit . . . perhaps the word I'm looking for is *unsteady.*"

"Well, if *you* don't know what word you're looking for," Phleg snapped, "*I* certainly don't." She didn't know what to make of all this. She had the feeling that although she understood all the individual words, she was still somehow missing the meaning. Sort of like with poetry. She had always suspected poets intentionally made up nonsense, just to feel superior to everyone else.

But if the *servant* was confused, that made everything more complicated. To prove she was steady—in case that *was* the word the servant was looking for—Phleg leaned over and picked up the wooden cup that had fallen off the night table. There was still some milk in it, and for some reason this was especially delicious milk. So Phleg drank down the last of it.

"Princess Gabriella!" the servant cried in horror.

Phleg sighed. She seemed to be getting everything wrong, and it was important that she be able to fit in. Her brother Parf had bet her that she'd never last three days. Phleg was determined not to lose that bet. "Was it yours?" Phleg asked.

"Certainly not!" the servant said. "But it was on the floor!"

"The cup was," Phleg pointed out. "Not the milk." Not that Phleg held anything against food that had been on the floor. But she probably wouldn't drink from the floor, no matter how sweet-tasting the milk was. Well . . . most likely not.

"I can get you more if you'd like," the servant offered. "And fresh. Maybe that would make you feel better."

"No, I'm done now." Phleg was eager to explore the castle,

10

where this princess whose place she had taken lived. She took a couple of long strides toward the door, noticing that the princess had longer legs than Phleg did, so she covered ground faster. Interesting.

"Princess Gabriella!" the servant once again cried.

"Now what?"

"You aren't dressed!"

Phleg looked down at herself in horror. The enchantment was supposed to have transformed her *exactly* into how the princess looked at the moment Phleg cast the spell, right down to her clothes.

And, indeed, she saw she was dressed in a lace-trimmed and beribboned white gown that looked just as Phleg thought a princess's dress *should* look.

"Of course I have clothes on," Phleg said, hoisting the garment up over her knees so that the servant could see the difference between *clothes on* and *clothes off.*

"Well, yes, certainly," the servant sputtered. "I didn't say you had *no* clothes on. I said you weren't dressed."

Phleg sighed impatiently, remembering the servant apparently didn't know all the words she should. "You're going to have to explain the difference to me."

"You're wearing your nightclothes."

"My what?"

"Your sleeping gown."

Phleg figured if she waited long enough, a better explanation would be offered.

Eventually, it was. Sort of. "Your gown for sleeping in."

Did the servant suspect she wasn't the real princess? Was this some sort of test? Phleg asked, "I have special clothes for sleeping in?"

The servant's relieved tone indicated she thought progress was being made. "Of course you do, Your Highness."

"Why?"

"So that your regular clothing doesn't get wrinkled and mussed."

Phleg looked down once again at the pretty princess dress she was wearing. "This isn't wrinkled," she said, smoothing it out over her thighs.

Looking as though she hated to disagree, the servant nodded and said, "But it is."

Phleg shrugged.

The servant said, "Perhaps I should summon the physician to take a look at that bump on your head after all."

Phleg had no idea why the woman was trying to change the subject. "No, you were right before: I'm fine."

"Well, then, should I help you get dressed?"

Phleg decided not to fight over every little thing. If people wore one set of clothes for sleeping in and another set of clothes for being awake in, she could do that. But then the servant's words sank in. "Help me get dressed?" she repeated.

The woman stepped forward and Phleg once again swatted her away. "Hands to yourself!" she commanded in the same tone she would use on her brothers.

The woman stepped back.

Phleg looked around the room, having no idea where the day clothes would be kept. Grudgingly she said, "Maybe you can fetch the clothes for me."

"Certainly, Your Highness."

And it was a good thing Phleg hadn't sent her from the room, because what an awful lot of clothes there were. "Those are all mine?" Phleg asked when the servant opened the door of a huge cupboard that held dozens of dresses, in all colors and an assortment of sparkliness.

"Certainly," the servant murmured.

Surely she wasn't expected to put them all on at once. She'd never be able to move with that many layers. "Hmmm," Phleg said, waiting for the servant to fill in the silence, to make things clearer.

Eventually she did. "Which one will you wear today?"

Phleg licked her lips nervously. Cagily, she announced, "This is a test: Which one do you *think* I should wear?"

"I would suggest . . ." The servant's hand hovered. "This sapphire-colored one that shows off your eyes so well."

"Just the one I was going to say," Phleg said. There was a mirror attached to the door of the cupboard, and Phleg caught sight of herself as Princess Gabriella. The princess did indeed have blue eyes, which seemed an oddly unbecoming shade to Phleg, since fairies have violet-colored eyes. And Princess Gabriella had dark brown hair that *obviously* hadn't been cut in ages, for it fell over her shoulders in gentle waves, whereas Phleg's hair was short and iridescent white and spiky. Phleg felt sorry for the princess. Here she had all these beautiful dresses, but they couldn't hide the fact that she was a big and galumphing human, and warthog ugly.

The servant had gone to other cupboards and was now pulling out more clothing.

"I thought I was going to wear the sapphire dress?" Phleg asked.

"Certainly. I'm just setting out your undergarments."

"*Under*garments," Phleg repeated. "That would be for . . ."

"Underneath," the servant finished for her.

"Hmmm," Phleg said again. "Better set them out in the order I'm meant to put them on."

"Certainly," the servant said. It seemed her favorite word. "And then, afterward, I can brush your hair for you."

Brush it? How would Princess Gabriella's hair ever come in spiky if it was brushed?

People! They were going to take some getting used to.

Chapter 2

The Complications of Complicated Families

PRINCESS GABRIELLA

Once the fairy children saw that Gabriella would not lose her patience and yell at or chase after them—or lose her nerve and break into dramatic weeping—they quickly grew bored.

"Wanna go pull the laundry lines down so the clothes fall into the dirt?" one of them suggested, and before Gabriella could say, "Oh, surely not!" the number of children went down from eleven—Gabriella had finally had the chance to count—to one. That one was the toddler of indeterminate gender. (Well, indeterminate to Gabriella. Presumably its family knew.) But the toddler couldn't keep up and was left behind, so it threw itself down on its well-padded bottom and began to wail.

One of the few subjects that had *not* been covered in Gabriella's education was the tending of babies, especially irate fairy babies whose faces were turning purple from screaming so hard.

"There, there," Gabriella said, and because she spoke so kindly and soothingly, the heartbroken child lifted its arms to her in a gesture even one unaccustomed to babies could recognize as the universal sign for *pick me up*.

"Oh," Gabriella said in a tone that—coming from anyone but a perfect princess—could almost be mistaken for a moan.

But, with tears still pouring down its cheeks, the child hiccuped what might have been the word *up*, so Gabriella took it in her arms, being careful of the tiny, delicate wings. She felt more unsure of herself now than she had since, at five years old, she was asked to be the judge at the countywide baking competition. She had needed to declare whose sugar cookies were better: those made by the mother of her best friend, Amanda (and they were scrumptious), or those made by the mean old wife of the miller (who'd put hazelnuts in hers, which was indisputably an inspired addition).

Safe in Gabriella's firm, if somewhat unenthusiastic, embrace, the fairy child stopped screeching, sniveling, or turning purple, and started playing with Gabriella's long, dark, wavy hair, so unlike that of its siblings. Gabriella forced herself not to think about how the child's fingers had been grimy to begin with and were now coated with tears and snot.

What Gabriella longed to do was to carry the child out of the room and find some adult fairies, in the hopes that she could:

1. hand over the child, and
2. talk them into returning her home, since this whole changeling episode had apparently been thought up by the children.

But she had been taken at night, and all she was wearing was her nightdress. True, it was cotton, not gauzy or see-through, and it covered her about as well as one of her summer dresses—and more than the fairy girls' dresses covered *them*. Still, it *was* a nightdress. There had been no protocol lesson to cover this, but she felt confident that princesses—even kidnapped-by-fairies princesses—should not wander around unknown places wearing only their nightclothes. Surely, *surely*, the children's mother would eventually come looking for the missing toddler. Or the missing Phleg.

So Gabriella sat down—on the floor (!)—and rocked the little one until it fell asleep, sucking on a strand of Gabriella's hair.

Still no adult fairies made an appearance.

What was going on at home? Surely no fairy—especially no fairy from *this* family—could pass for her, even if magically altered to wear Gabriella's form. Not for a moment.

Well . . .

Gabriella had to admit to herself that the servants might not like to rush to judgment. But her father would definitely notice.

Well . . . assuming his duties as head of state didn't keep him away.

In which case her mother . . . her mother . . .

While Gabriella had to admit her mother was often distracted by her royal social obligations, she *would* know. If not immediately, soon.

Soonish.

Sooner or later.

Eventually . . .

But not to worry. Amanda, who'd been Gabriella's friend since they were as young as this indeterminate fairy child, *Amanda* could be counted on to raise the alarm within moments of meeting the false Gabriella. *She* would see, and she would not rest until the king and queen were convinced. In fact, a search was probably already under way. Gabriella would be rescued in no time.

Meanwhile, however, Gabriella had nothing to do but to study her surroundings. She might be in a tower, judging by the curve of the walls, which were constructed of stone like the walls of her parents' castle. But these were stones of sparkly pastel colors. Very pretty, she had to admit. And yet there was only one window, in the ceiling. Didn't it ever rain here where the fairies lived? Even if there were shutters on the outside— which she could not see any evidence of—surely some water would drip in. That might have explained why the room was bare except for the piles of straw that apparently served as sleeping mats: no chests for clothing, nor any place to store possessions of any sort. No nightstand to hold cups of milk, even for the youngest. The heaps of straw were more *scattered* than arranged into neat piles. Despite her annoyance with the fairies— which Gabriella was too well-bred to let show—she felt sorry for them, thinking that even the peasants in her father's kingdom had more.

Eventually the child awoke, hungry apparently, for it started crying again, and stuffing fistfuls of Gabriella's hair into its mouth.

This will not do, Gabriella told herself. The child must be attended to, despite the risk to her own royal dignity.

So, tucking the squalling child beneath her arm, Gabriella marched out of the room—and straight into the only fairy whose name she knew: Parf.

Not sure whether she was a prisoner who was supposed to stay put and would be punished otherwise, she immediately explained about the baby. "He's hungry."

She said *he* because *it* sounded insulting, and she had a fifty-fifty chance of being right.

But also a fifty-fifty chance of being wrong.

"*He?*" Parf said blankly, despite the fact that she'd made to hand the toddler to him. Her meaning had to be clear.

"Excuse me," she said without a trace of sarcasm. She cleared her throat, as though it was dryness that had made her intended word come out sounding wrong. "I meant to say *she's* hungry."

Parf snorted, not fooled for an instant. "Dumb twit of a human girl," he scoffed, which was not an acceptable thing to say in any social circumstance. But he did take the child. And he seemed perfectly capable of distracting his little sister by bouncing her.

"What," Gabriella asked him, "is my status?"

"Your what?"

Gabriella suspected Parf didn't know the word. "My position," she clarified. "My standing."

"Well, that's it exactly," Parf told her. "Your position is that you're standing." He held the tot up so that they were face-to-face. "Isn't she the stupidest human girl?" he cooed to the child. "Yes, she is. Indeed she is."

Gabriella took a steadying breath. "I am not stupid," she said—not arguing, just clarifying. "I simply do not understand what's expected. I've never had experience being . . ." She wasn't sure if there was such a word. ". . . changelinged."

"Well, duh," Parf said. "Phleg took your place, you took hers. Didn't I tell you this already?"

"Yes, but . . ."

"So you take over Phleg's chores."

"Oh." So apparently she wasn't meant to be held captive in the children's bedchamber. But . . . chores? She suspected this did not mean judging baking contests or declaring spring officially started or dancing with the ambassadors who came to her father's court. She could have refused to cooperate, but that didn't seem the princessly thing to do. Besides, she didn't want to anger the fairies in case they *might* confine her to one room. "What sort of chores does Phleg do?" Gabriella asked.

"Miss-mot," he announced, looking very pleased with himself.

"I don't know what that is," she admitted.

"Not *what*: *who*." Parf grinned, and handed the baby back to her. He waved his hand in front of his nose. "Which includes diaper duty."

Of course.

But before Gabriella could point out all the ways in which she was unqualified for this task, she heard what could only be a howl of rage come from not too far away. Anxiously, she tried to determine from which direction the noise had erupted. Impossible to tell. She and Parf were standing in a room whose

20

sole function seemed to be to give access to other places. Like the sleeping chamber, this room was also shaped in a perfect circle, and there were six doorways—all the doors were open—including one that led to the outside, showing grass just beyond. She was not high up in a tower after all.

In another instant, some (if not all, for they were too fast for her to be sure) of the fairy children came tearing in, separating and diving through various doorways.

More angry howls. Coming closer.

Gabriella saw that Parf, though looking grim, was standing his ground. "What—?" she started. But that was the only word she had time to get out before a new fairy strode into the entryway, one she hadn't met before.

This fairy was an adult. Gabriella could tell, though it would have been hard to say how she knew. The newcomer was no taller than Parf. It wasn't that her face was lined—and of course they all had that silver-white hair—but something about her features and the way she held herself gave the impression that she was older. And furious.

"Don't think you can get away from me, you little brats!" the woman screamed at the open doors, shaking the piece of hyacinth-colored fabric she clutched.

Parf looked at Gabriella. "Not *what*," he told her once again. "*Who*." Then, turning to the adult fairy, he greeted her. "Hello, Mumsy."

"Don't *Mumsy* me!" the older fairy snapped. "I spent all morning washing the laundry, and somebody—*somebody*—has snipped the drying lines so that everything—*everything*—needs to be cleaned again." She flung the offending skirt onto the floor and stomped on it. *"Everything!"*

Gabriella gasped. She had heard the plan, but she had never considered that the children could be plotting against their own mother.

The mother, Mumsy, glared at her. "Who in the wide world are you?" she demanded, which is not a good welcoming speech, no matter the circumstances.

Still, Gabriella curtseyed. "Princess Gabriella of Fairhaven, daughter of King Humphrey and Queen—"

"Nobody cares," the fairy mother interrupted. By not introducing herself, she forced Gabriella to continue thinking of her as "Mumsy."

Parf stepped in. "Gabby is taking Phleg's place." He lowered his voice to add, "I think she may well have egged the others on."

Gabriella couldn't even get her mouth to work.

Fortunately, Mumsy knew her children better than that. "And you," she said to Parf, "no doubt tried valiantly to stop them." But then she turned her attention back to Gabriella. "Just what I need!" she cried. "Another mouth to feed." She looked the human girl up and down. "And you're enormous," she said. Again, it was a phrase for which there is no correct social occasion. "I'll bet you eat twice as much as any one of my children."

Helpfully, Parf said, "But she'll be able to reach higher, so she can help with more chores."

"I beg your pardon," Gabriella said.

"*More chores*," Parf repeated loudly. To Mumsy, he explained, "Gabby's a bit hard of hearing, and more than a bit slow."

"I ... I ...," Gabriella stammered. "My name is Gabriella, not Gabby." This was not being confrontational. This was simply setting the record straight.

"Fine," Mumsy said to Parf, totally ignoring Gabriella's protests. "She can start with redoing the laundry and fixing the lines." She sniffed. "After she changes the baby's diaper."

"Yes, Mumsy," Parf said.

Mumsy shook her head and started for one of the doorways. "I don't know what's the matter with you children," she said. "You act as though you were raised by wolves."

"You should know," Parf muttered after her.

"What?" Mumsy asked.

Parf shifted to a totally different tone. "You should know," he repeated, "that I will keep Gabby on task."

Clearly not fooled, Mumsy narrowed her violet eyes at him and shook her head. "Raised by wolves," she repeated.

PHLEG

The servant's name was Ellen. She told that to Phleg the fourth or fifth time Phleg called her *Hey, you*.

"Perhaps your memory has been affected by that bump to your head," Ellen suggested as she set out the princess clothing Phleg was to wear.

"Well," Phleg pointed out, "*Ellen* is a very hard name to remember."

"Indeed," Ellen murmured.

At first Phleg thought Princess Gabriella must be the stupidest princess in the world to need a servant to get her dressed, but in the end, Phleg had to accept Ellen's help, not only for the proper order, but also to get all the fasteners fastened, laces laced, and buttons buttoned.

"This undergarment is itchy," Phleg complained, scratching loudly at the stiff fabric.

"Yes," Ellen admitted, even though the sound of Phleg's scratching made her wince, "but not so much once you put the dress on over it, and it will make the dress poof away from you *so* becomingly."

"I suppose I can try," Phleg grumbled.

Ellen wrestled the dress onto Phleg. "There!" she exclaimed, as though enthusiasm would cure everything.

"Still itchy," Phleg said.

"So I see." Ellen seemed to be having a hard time convincing her own hands not to take hold of Phleg's hands. "I do believe you'll get used to it, Princess Gabriella. You *have* worn this on other occasions, and it never seemed to bother you before."

"Perhaps the bump on my head has made my skin more sensitive," Phleg suggested, using the servant's own argument.

"Perhaps," Ellen agreed. "And perhaps, also, you might . . ." She couldn't bring herself to use the word *scratch* in front of royalty, so she just gestured with her fingers. ". . . be a bit more discreet."

"What do you mean?" asked Phleg, who had hoisted up the skirt of the dress to get at the itch under her ribs.

Ellen must have realized she had to make concessions. She once again gestured with her fingers. "*Over* the garments," she said, "and if at all possible, not quite so . . . vigorously." In a clear attempt to distract the princess, she added, "And here are your beautiful shoes."

Phleg liked that they sparkled, but as soon as she put them on, she said, "They pinch."

"No, they don't," Ellen said, beginning to lose patience.

"They're not your toes," Phleg pointed out, even though strictly speaking they weren't *hers*, either.

"I meant," Ellen said, "they never pinched before."

"Perhaps the bump to my head . . . ," Phleg started.

". . . has caused your toes to swell?" Ellen finished.

"Odder things have happened," Phleg said. She slipped off a shoe for a closer inspection. "What are they made of?" she asked. The fairies used leaves that had been shaped and strengthened with enchantments.

"Leather from a newborn calf," Ellen told her.

It was the *newborn* that for a moment confounded Phleg. It almost seemed to imply that the leather was something the calf had grown out of, like baby teeth. But *snakes* shed their skins, not *cows*. Phleg let the one shoe drop and hurriedly kicked off the other, forcefully enough that it bounced off a wall. "You mean they're made of dead animals? You want me to wear dead animals on my feet?"

"No . . . ," Ellen said uncertainly.

An awful thought occurred to Phleg, and a possible explanation for the itchiness of the unfamiliar clothing. She put her hands up to the neckline of her dress, ready to rip it off. "Is this a dead animal, too?"

"No," Ellen assured her. "The undergarments are starched linen, and the dress itself is wool."

Phleg tried to process this. "Linen comes from . . . ?"

"From flax."

"Flax is a plant," Phleg said, "so that's all right. Wool . . ." Her eyes grew wide with shock. "Wool is from sheep!"

"Living sheep," Ellen hurried to assure her. "Their coats are sheared, which doesn't hurt them any more than getting your hair cut hurts you."

Considering how long the princess's hair was, Phleg doubted if Gabriella had any personal experience with getting her hair cut. "You have strange customs," Phleg said, then caught herself and corrected that to, "We. We have strange customs. I've often wondered about them."

"Hmmm," Ellen said, not sounding convinced. "So are you going to put the shoes back on?"

"No," Phleg said. "I can go around in bare feet."

"You most certainly can*not*." For a moment, Ellen sounded more like a mother than a servant. She put her hands on her hips and looked Phleg directly in the eye. Then she seemed to remember she was a serving maid, talking to a royal. "You may, however, wear some of your house slippers," she said more diffidently. "*They* are made from wool."

26

The slippers were blue-and-gold brocade, a softer blue than her dress, which Ellen seemed to think made them only barely appropriate. But besides being made of something that wasn't dead animal, they didn't pinch.

"There!" Phleg said. "That was a chore, wasn't it! Now what?"

"Now," Ellen said, sounding a bit weary, though it was still only early morning, "breakfast."

Phleg's stomach rumbled at the thought of food. Ellen pretended not to hear, though her face showed she had. "Where's that?" Phleg asked.

"Where's what?"

"Where's breakfast?"

"The solarium. Same as every other morning."

Phleg pointed to her head as an excuse for not knowing. And pointed again when she needed to ask, "And, remind me, where's the solarium?"

Ellen sighed. Loudly. "I'll take you."

This was a good decision, as the castle the princess lived in was vast, much larger than the home Phleg had left behind. And filled with so many things! She would have to remember everything so she could gloat to her siblings about all she'd seen. (Wouldn't last three days, indeed!) There were tables and cupboards and mirrors and bookcases and vases with flowers, and stairs to go up and down, and rugs to be careful not to trip over. Being taller than she was used to, Phleg had trouble gauging exactly how high doorways and ceilings were, and how many strides it would take to get across a space. As a consequence she repeatedly ducked, convinced she couldn't possibly fit through

27

doorways that proved perfectly adequate to allow passage to even a whopping big princess, and she kept stubbing her toes against the legs of pieces of furniture.

"Too bad you're wearing those light slippers instead of regular shoes," Ellen observed, after one such collision made Phleg yowl in pain and exasperation. "Dead animals go a long way toward protecting feet."

"It's not nice to make fun of someone with a bumped head," Phleg told her.

By the time they got to the solarium, they were told they had just missed the king, who had needed to get about his daily duties. These included taking someone called Leopold on a hunting trip. (*More dead animals*, Phleg noted.)

The queen was just about ready to leave, too. If Phleg could pull this off, the queen would be her mumsy for the next three days. Still, she seemed more like Aunt Sylvimit than Mumsy, as she was dressed very elegantly and didn't look at all tired out and ready to bite someone's head off. Nor did she say, *If you're going to be late for a meal, then I guess you aren't all that hungry.* What she said was a bright, "There you are, Gabriella," accompanied by a kiss that missed Phleg's cheek by at least the width of a hand. That was *very* Aunt Sylvimit. "I'll see you later, as our schedules permit."

"Sure," Phleg said, feeling slightly relieved. Fooling a mother would be the hardest task a changeling could face.

And she was right to be concerned: Even her one-word response was enough to make the queen pause on her way out of the room. "Are you quite all right, darling?"

28

"I bumped my head."

This was the wrong thing to say, as far as getting the queen to leave. "Oh, you poor dear." Gabriella's mother came and peered closely at Phleg's face, gently brushing the long hair away from her forehead. "It doesn't look very bad."

"It's not," Phleg assured her, because it wasn't—but also so that she would leave.

"Well, you just take it easy today," the queen advised. "Ellen will arrange with the secretary to take everything off your schedule." She kissed Phleg again, and this time her lips actually made contact with skin. "You just sit here with Amanda as long as you want, and do whatever the two of you wish." She lowered her voice as though sharing a secret. "It will be a day off."

Not trusting words, since she'd apparently aroused suspicion already, Phleg nodded. She didn't ask who Amanda was, as there was a girl who looked about her own age who was sitting at the table grinning at her. Phleg nodded at her, too, for good measure.

The queen took a moment longer before removing the hand she held so gently against Phleg's cheek, but then she had to go, trailed by the majority of the people who'd been in the room with her, leaving only Phleg, Ellen, and Amanda.

"Is there anything more you need, Your Highness?" Ellen asked Phleg. "Or shall I see about rearranging your schedule?"

Phleg nodded again, since she'd been having such good luck with that. After a moment's hesitation, Ellen took the gesture to mean the latter, and she too left.

Was this Amanda who was sitting at the table another servant? Phleg decided not, as serving staff entered the room bearing trays of pastries, and warm buttered bread, and eggs, and a pitcher of what looked to be that same delicious sweet milk that she'd had in her room. Not one of them took a seat at the table. Amanda must be a guest. Probably one of the real Princess Gabriella's friends.

"Your Highness?" asked the server carrying the pastries.

Phleg nodded.

Which, in this case, was apparently the wrong answer. The man quirked an eyebrow at her. "Which would you like?"

Did he mean she had to choose only one of the pastries, or did she have to choose between pastries, warm bread, and eggs? In either case, this made no sense, as there were no brothers and sisters who needed sharing with.

She said, "I'll take them all."

"One of each?" he asked.

"All."

The servers scurried to make room in front of her, and set down their heaping trays, arrayed in all their glory before her.

"Well done," Amanda whispered at her as the servers left, and for a moment Phleg thought she meant in selecting all the food. But then she saw that Amanda had only one piece of buttered bread on her plate. Had she eaten all the rest of her food already?

Phleg gave Amanda the same quirked eyebrow look the server had given her.

"Getting out of your lessons and speeches and meetings and

so forth," Amanda clarified. "I have to admit: I didn't really believe you'd do it."

"Do what?" Phleg asked, but she was distracted by all those pastries. She picked up a fruit tart that was about as big around as the palm of her hand. She suspected that if she bit it, it would crumble and flake, and pieces would end up falling on her. So she popped the whole thing in her mouth.

Amanda averted her gaze from the sight of Phleg chewing and explained, "I never thought you'd make an excuse to get out of your regularly scheduled tasks."

When Phleg didn't answer, making delighted-sounding moans over the deliciousness of the tart instead, Amanda added, "As I suggested."

Phleg rolled her tongue over her teeth to make sure there were no tasty crumbs hiding between them and her lips.

Amanda said, "In that note I slipped under your door this morning."

Phleg plucked a roll that had icing on the top and popped that into her mouth. Custard squished out from the middle, some making it as far away as her chin before Phleg's tongue retrieved it. "Mmm!" she cried. Then she added, speaking around the custard, "Didn't see a note."

Amanda was fanning herself with a square of cloth, looking somewhat faint. These people who lived at the castle must be delicate that way, for squares of cloth had been provided by each place setting at the table. Still, Amanda seemed to be taking news of the lost note very hard.

Phleg explained, "I fell out of bed this morning, and my servant, Ellen, came in to help me get dressed. Maybe your note got shoved under something in all the commotion." She nodded her chin toward Amanda's breakfast, where the butter that had dripped off her toast was beginning to congeal on the plate. "You going to eat that?" she asked.

"Be my guest," Amanda said. Her voice sounded oddly strained, making Phleg wonder if she *had* been planning to eat. But if so, wouldn't she just have warned, *Hands off?*

Phleg gobbled down the bread quickly, just in case Amanda was reconsidering, then licked the plate. "So what did this note say?" she asked, scooping a handful of the scrambled eggs out of the bowl. "This is good stuff. Want some?"

Amanda shook her head. She seemed to be having difficulty maintaining her train of thought. Probably, Phleg estimated, because she didn't eat enough. "Uhm, I wrote to tell you that I heard Prince Frederic isn't going on the hunt with the other men. That means we might have a chance to see him today. In the gardens. Without a chaperone."

"Well, that is good news," Phleg said, since Amanda seemed to think so, despite the fact that at the moment her face was turning an interesting shade of green as she watched Phleg eat. Phleg drank some of the milk—which was every bit as good as her first impression of it had been—then she wiped her mouth with her sleeve. "So who's this Fred person?" she asked.

Amanda only looked at her without saying a word.

"Don't know?" Phleg asked her. "Just heard the name and figured I'd be interested?"

Amanda had to try twice before she got her mouth and her vocal cords coordinated. "Prince Frederic," Amanda finally got out, "is the young man to whom you're betrothed."

Betrothed? Princess Gabriella was scheduled to get married? Not in the next three days, Phleg hoped. That would nudge the situation beyond complicated all the way into disastrous.

Phleg nodded solemnly. "Yes indeedy," she told Amanda. "I'm glad to see you're up to date on these things. Well done. I bet you even know *when*."

"Of course not," Amanda snapped. "Nobody does. The date hasn't been set yet."

"Ha!" Phleg said. "Trick question! Couldn't trick *you*, though." She took a big gulp of milk as an excuse to stop talking.

Perhaps a bit *too* big a gulp.

Phleg couldn't figure out about the white cloth covering the table. She had already deduced that the smaller cloths set to the side of each dish were there in case someone needed to fan herself, given that people—at least castle people—seemed highly strung and excitable and in frequent need of fanning. But the big cloth had the dishes sitting on it, so you had to lean way down in order to blow your nose into it if—as had just occurred with Phleg—you happened to gulp your milk too quickly and started coughing and sneezing.

And now the princess's friend Amanda slammed her hand down on the table, forcefully enough that the nearest dishes and utensils bounced, and the spoon that was in the bowl of scrambled eggs flipped up and out, splattering egg onto the white cloth. Very impractical, that white cloth.

Phleg slid her hand under the gooey eggy glob and helpfully stuffed it into her mouth, so that the only evidence left on the cloth was a yellow stain rather than actual foodstuffs.

Rather than thanking her, Amanda made a gagging sound. If she was feeling unwell, that explained why she was not eating. But it didn't explain the hand slamming. "What is the matter with you?" Amanda demanded. "I have never seen you in such a peculiar and contrary mood."

It was way, *way* too early for people to be getting suspicious. Phleg had been impersonating the princess for not even one morning long. How would she ever last three days at this rate? And she'd been doing such a good job. She considered what she might do to set the girl's doubts to rest. This was difficult, given that Phleg didn't know why Amanda was suspicious. So Phleg decided to admit her ignorance: She said, "Dunno."

Amanda sighed. Loudly. "Be that way," she snapped.

So that was good. "All right," Phleg said, since agreeing was the opposite of being contrary.

But, then again, maybe not.

Amanda slapped the table once again, though this time the utensils stayed mostly put. Alerted either by Amanda's raised voice or the rattling cutlery, one of the servants was approaching from his station by the door, where he was positioned so as not to intrude on mealtime conversation. Amanda waved him away before he got there, then she leaned closer to hiss at Phleg, "I'm supposed to be your best friend. You're supposed to tell me everything."

"Um . . ."

Clearly Amanda was waiting for more.

So Phleg continued, "You are. I do," even though she wasn't exactly sure what a best friend was. Her family kept to themselves for the most part, meaning she knew more relatives than unrelated fairies. Phleg would be hard pressed to say which of her siblings or cousins or aunts or uncles was the least annoying, never mind which she liked best.

"What's going on?" Amanda demanded.

"I'm eating," Phleg explained. "And you're not." Clearly Amanda was slow, and allowances needed to be made. Phleg spoke one word at a time, loudly and distinctly. "I thought, once we finished, we were going to spy on that Fred person you mentioned. But I don't know what you plan to do with the information you get from watching him." Phleg and her brothers and sisters sometimes spied on each other. If they were lucky, they learned things they could use against one another.

Amanda stood. "I never said anything about spying on Prince Frederic."

Phleg didn't ask why, then, they should be interested. She said, "I'm not quite finished eat—"

Amanda cut her off. "I shall be with my mother and the other ladies-in-waiting when you're feeling more yourself." She strode away from the table, slamming the door as she left.

What an odd thing to say, Phleg thought. Who else would anyone feel like *except* herself?

She glanced at the servant who'd gone back to his place by the door. He raised his eyebrows ever so slightly, which may or may not have meant that he, too, thought Amanda's actions were mystifying.

35

Phleg shrugged and finished eating all the eggs and toast and pastries that had been set out on the table, including Amanda's cup of milk.

The servant approached and asked, "Should I get more from the kitchen, Princess Gabriella?"

Startled, Phleg looked over her shoulder, but then remembered *she* was Princess Gabriella for the time being, and the man was talking to her. "*Is* there more?" she asked.

"Whatever you want," the servant assured her, "whenever you want it."

Whenever . . .

"There's enough for the midday meal?" she asked.

The man blinked, but otherwise his expression didn't change. "Of course, my lady. Supper, also."

"Of course," she repeated, as a princess might. "That's as it should be. I'm through for now."

"Very good, my lady." He pulled her chair away from the table, which was a favorite trick of her brothers, so Phleg saw it coming. She jumped to her feet so that she didn't fall off.

"Where should I go now?" she asked.

"Wherever you want, my lady."

Where did someone who didn't have to cook and clean and do laundry and tend to both animals and younger siblings—where did such a person go?

Amanda had said she was going to be with the ladies-in-waiting but had not explained what they were waiting for. Generally, Phleg didn't like waiting, and besides, Amanda seemed too moody. It was hard to guess what Princess Gabriella saw in her.

But Amanda had also said Fred-who-was-betrothed-to-Princess-Gabriella was going to be in the garden.

"I will go to the garden," Phleg announced.

"Very good, my lady."

"Of course it's good," Phleg said. "I wouldn't have decided it otherwise. Only . . ."

"My lady?"

Phleg considered. She must act like a princess, so as not to arouse suspicion. "Of course, because I am the princess, I know where the garden is. I know where it is so well that I could give anyone directions on how to get there. But I'm wondering if you, as a servant, are able to give other people, maybe people who might be visiting the castle for the first time, good directions."

The servant looked somewhat befuddled, but he got over it quickly. "The garden is by the west wing of the castle, my lady."

"No, no," she said. "Pretend I don't know where anything is. Pretend I'm standing here, and I'm a first-time visitor, and I want to go to the garden. Which is . . . where . . . exactly?"

Any of her siblings would have said *outside*, but the servant was more helpful. He directed her to the door that was best to leave by (the room had four doors to choose from), and how many doorways she then had to pass before turning right. He even indicated with a small flick of his hand which direction *right* was, just in case she had trouble remembering. Then he

37

instructed her to head down the stairs. The open doorway to outside would be directly in front of her.

There was a whole other set of directions for once she was outside.

"Very good," Phleg said. "You know your directions well, especially considering how many rooms this castle has."

"Your father is a wealthy man," the servant told her.

The comment took Phleg by surprise, since most people—including Mumsy—called her father an idle loser. But in a moment she had caught up: The servant was talking about the king, Princess Gabriella's father. She had to keep her mind from wandering, lest she say something unprincesslike and give herself away.

"Well," she said, "toodles." That was how her aunt, Mumsy's sister, said good-bye. And Phleg's Aunt Sylvimit was the most refined member the family had.

Phleg counted the doorways correctly, made it down the stairs without tripping, and succeeded in finding the outside. She had some trouble determining which was the "really big tree" the servant had told her about—obviously, the man had not spent much time in the deep woods—but eventually she found the garden.

Somehow or other she missed the pergola entrance that the servant had described, with its honeysuckle climbing up the latticework arch, so she had to squeeze in between a cluster of lavender and a rhododendron to make it onto the path. The garden was much too ordered for Phleg's taste, with gillyflowers in pots rather than allowed to vine where they would, but she knew that was the way people liked things. The colors weren't as bright to her human eyes as they would have been to her fairy eyes, and the fragrances not as strong as she would have expected, but it was still all so lovely that for a while she forgot why she had come.

Then she heard voices, and she remembered she had come in order to spy on Gabriella's Fred.

Moving carefully, so as not to alert anyone to her presence, she determined that the voices came from where the path curved around a towering wild rosebush. Phleg crept closer, then sat down on the ground behind it and peered through the thorny branches, to watch without being seen.

Sitting on a stone bench were a young man just a bit older than her—probably about Parf's age—and a boy who was closer to five or six. The older one had to be Prince Fred, as Amanda had said he and Princess Gabriella were betrothed. Phleg knew that sometimes, in the world of people as well as in the fairy world, two kings would make an alliance by declaring an upcoming marriage between the son of one and the daughter of the other. The declaration could be made while the children were still . . . well, children, with the actual marriage to take place once both were of age. But Phleg guessed that Amanda wouldn't have sounded so excited at the prospect of Princess Gabriella getting a chance to meet her betrothed if he was a five-year-old.

The boys had to be brothers, as they were bigger and smaller versions of each other. Their hair was not quite as dark brown as Gabriella's, and curly, like the coat of a sheep. Despite the hair, she supposed Fred was attractive—for a person—although she knew she would never get used to how freakishly tall people were.

Fred was the one who was doing the talking at the moment, with his brother listening intently. Fred was saying something about someone named Telmund, describing a fight with a band of wicked pirates, with much swordplay and wordplay and leaping about in dramatic stances—which Fred would sometimes jump to his feet to demonstrate, and the brother to imitate. Phleg was skeptical that any of this had much to do with the way a real encounter with pirates would go.

Fred was telling his brother a story.

The way the younger boy was sitting on the edge of his seat showed how caught up he was in the unlikely goings-on. Also, whenever he spoke the hero's name, there was something about the way he said it that made Phleg suspect that hero and little brother shared the same name.

Even without the hook of the hero being named after her, Phleg found that Fred's words captured her, too. He might have hair like a sheep, but he could tell a good story. She could hear the sails snapping in the wind. She could taste the sea spray on her lips, feel the heaving of the deck beneath her feet. Then . . .

"Oh no!" brother-Telmund cried. Story-Telmund, having been disarmed by the pirate king—through treachery rather than skill—now stood with the pirate's blade pressed against his throat.

Here it is, Phleg thought, sure of what was coming. She was disappointed, for she wanted the adventure to continue.

If Parf could tell a tale so well, which he could not, this would be the moment he'd strike. Having engaged his younger siblings in the story so that all else was forgotten—having made them care about the hero so much that he seemed more real than reality—*that* was when Parf would say: "And so the pirate swung his sword, taking off the hero's head, which bounced twice across the deck of the pirate ship, then once more and overboard, where the waiting sharks devoured it, so that all the prisoners he had come to rescue ended up spending the rest of their short, miserable lives as the pirates' slaves. The end."

The siblings would cry and have nightmares for days.

But that wasn't what Fred said. Fred said that Telmund grabbed one of the lines hanging from the yardarm, then swung himself up into the pirate ship's rigging.

Could someone do that? Who cared? Phleg was relieved he had.

And this was when Phleg realized that Fred understood his listener as thoroughly as Parf knew his, but that Fred used his knowledge to bring his brother *just* to the edge of real fear, and then he would back off, for his intention clearly was not to scare, but to entertain.

She could let go and allow Fred's words to sweep her away.

Eventually, the hero Telmund overcame the pirate king, and his bravery and his good humor and his innocence won over the rest of the crew, and they were sailing back to a safe harbor when a sudden gale blew them off course and straight into another adventure.

41

Phleg was enthralled by the story every bit as much as the younger brother was, so that she gradually realized she was coming to fall in love with the bold adventurer, whom she pictured as a fairy, though admittedly one who had Fred's face—minus the silly hair, of course. And maybe she could imagine the hero a little bit taller than the average fairy.

She was so entranced by the hero's deeds that she was totally unaware of the passage of time. She was also totally unaware of one of the castle servants coming up behind her until the woman gasped, "Princess Gabriella! Oh, somebody help! Princess Gabriella has fallen!"

It took several moments to come back to the real world. Phleg had, without realizing she was doing it, come to be lying belly-down on the ground to better watch the boys through the lower branches of the rosebush. Her elbows were in the dirt, her chin resting on her hands.

Ellen, Phleg remembered, even as she made gestures to shush the woman.

Too late. Fred had stopped speaking, and his little brother had catapulted himself off the bench and now stood in front of the bush, bobbing, trying to catch sight of her.

"I'm fine," Phleg whispered. She wished she could turn back time to before she'd been discovered, so that the story could continue. But she could not. She slapped away Ellen's fluttering hands. Louder, she said, "Leave me alone."

By the time she got to her feet—without Ellen's help—she saw that Fred had also stood. He was tall enough to look over the shrubbery at her.

"Princess Gabriella," he said, sounding as flustered as Phleg felt. "I didn't realize it was you listening."

He had seen her? Of course he had. She realized Fred would have been able to glimpse the blue of her sapphire-colored dress through the brown branches, green leaves, and white flowers of the bush.

"Yes," Phleg admitted, "it was me."

He stammered, "I—I assumed you were one of the serving girls. I would have invited you to join us had I known . . . Are you all right?"

"Well," Phleg told him, "I'm not, you didn't, and I am."

Young Telmund, who couldn't see her over the branches of the rosebush, had moved to stand in front of the hydrangeas next to it, which were shorter. He used his arm to brush some of them aside so that he could gawk at her.

Phleg looked down and saw that her pretty gown had grass and dirt stains on the front. She'd never before been concerned about such things, but now she made to brush the dirt away. At the last moment she instead waved her hand in the dismissive way she thought a princess might. "Carry on," she told the boys, then asked Ellen, "What *do* you want?"

"Richard sent me to find you," Ellen explained. She restrained herself from tending to Phleg's dress, but just barely. Before Phleg could ask who Richard was, Ellen continued, "He said you seemed quite interested in lunch before you asked for directions to the garden."

Lunch must be people's name for the midday meal, as the other meal the servant had mentioned, *supper*, would be the

43

evening meal. "I did not," Phleg protested, "ask for directions to the garden. I am the princess here. How could I *not* know my way to the garden?"

"Is that a trick question?" Ellen asked.

Ellen's question itself sounded like a trick question. Phleg changed the subject. "So is it time for lunch?" Could she have been so wrapped up in Fred's story about Telmund that she'd lost track of that much time?

Apparently, for Ellen was nodding.

"Well, then, let's go." Following Ellen would be easier than finding her own way back.

Still, it was difficult to leave without looking back at Fred and his brother and wondering what new story she would miss.

Chapter 3

A Bad Start

PRINCESS GABRIELLA

"Well," Parf told Gabriella, while he continued to bounce his baby sister to keep her from fussing, "you better get a move on."

"I'm sorry: I have no idea what you're saying," Gabriella replied, though she had a sinking feeling she might.

"Those clothes need rewashing. And the day's only getting hotter. You might be thankful for that while you're actually riverside, knee-deep in the washing, but you're gonna wish for the early morning cool while you're lugging all that wet laundry up the hill, where the clothes are hung to catch the breeze."

He seemed to be saying *you* an awful lot. In the I'm-so-interested tones she'd use at a state dinner, Gabriella said, without letting any sarcasm seep through, "You sound like an expert in matters of laundry. You must help your mother and your sister often."

"Naw," Parf said. "I just hear a lot about it, 'cause they're both loud complainers."

Gabriella smiled apologetically. "Well, unfortunately I'm not going to be able to help, either." She said *help* even though she suspected the plan was that she do it entirely on her own. At home, there was an army of servants whose sole function was the gathering of soiled garments and linens, followed by the washing, hanging, taking down, and folding of laundry. There was a whole other set of servants in charge of heating and applying the smoothing stones used to remove creases and wrinkles, and a master presser who was an expert at setting pleats. Gabriella had many duties as a princess, but laundry was not one of them.

Parf protested her lack of enthusiasm with a bit of a whine to his voice: "Mumsy said."

The baby, Miss-mot, caught his unhappy tone and began whining herself.

Gabriella's diplomacy teacher always stressed respect for different cultures. Traveling to foreign lands was a privilege, he'd told her on many occasions, and the one unforgivable crime of tourism was to act superior, as though one's own customs had more value than those of other people. Gabriella doubted the man had laundry on his mind when he'd said that, nor was she entirely convinced that being magicked away to the home of rude fairies counted as travel, but it was generally better to err on the side of friendliness. So she explained to Parf, "But I only have this nightdress. According to social convention, I shouldn't have left the bedchamber wearing only this, and I definitely can't go outdoors in such a state." Perhaps a bit of sarcasm came through as she asked, "This washing river *is* outdoors, isn't it?"

Parf waved her objections away as though they were a bad odor. Or maybe he actually *was* waving away a bad odor, considering Miss-mot's soggy clothing. "You look fine," he assured Gabriella—as though that was what she had said.

"And . . ." Gabriella lifted her foot so that it would show beneath the hem of the nightdress. "No shoes."

Parf sighed and opened one of the doors. This did not lead to another room, but to a wardrobe. There were five shelves, which held some, though not many, articles of jumbled clothing. They were small, even given the fairies' diminutive size. Gabriella guessed that this must be where Miss-mot's clothing was stored. Everything looked too small to fit anyone else. Out of the basket beneath the lowest shelf, Parf plucked two tiny shoes and handed them to Gabriella.

"*She* doesn't need shoes," Gabriella said. "*I* do."

Parf gave a throaty sigh of exasperation. "Are all humans as slooooow as you?"

That was a question that had a variety of answers, but none of which her diplomacy teacher would approve. So Gabriella said nothing, just looked at the infuriatingly offensive fairy boy.

"They stretch." Parf tugged on one of the shoes, demonstrating.

"Oh," Gabriella said. "I didn't know." *Don't say it. Don't say it,* she warned herself, but she couldn't help thinking: *There was no way I COULD know.*

She took one of the shoes. It was eggplant purple, not—to Gabriella's fashion sense—a suitable shade for footwear.

Miss-mot giggled and reached for the shoe.

Gabriella let the toddler take it, thinking, *Better her than me.*

But Miss-mot didn't want to *wear* the shoe, she wanted to suck on it.

With a how-could-you-be-so-stupid? look at Gabriella, Parf took the shoe away from his sister—who began to wail in protest—and handed it back to Gabriella.

Gabriella shook off the baby spit, then tugged at heel and toe and was eventually able to wedge her foot into it, though it was a tight squeeze. "I think I need a bigger size," she said, and tactfully refrained from adding, *And a more appealing color.*

"They only come in one size," Parf told her. "One size fits everybody."

"Apparently not me."

"That's only because you have absurdly big feet."

"I—" Gabriella cut off a rebuttal. "Fine. I'll make do."

"Good for you!" Parf, who had clearly never had a diplomacy teacher, made no attempt to disguise *his* sarcasm. He picked up a wrinkled doll-sized dress that was marigold yellow, not a color Gabriella felt flattered many.

"For me?" she asked, trying not to let her distaste show.

Parf gave her a you-are-so-tiresome look. "Do you need slits for your wings?"

Gabriella didn't bother to point out that she hadn't noticed the design, meant to accommodate fairy wings.

"Besides, our clothes can't stretch *that* much," Parf snorted. "And stop always thinking about yourself! I already told you what you're wearing ain't half bad. You need to change Miss-mot before you see about the laundry."

48

Selfish people always and only think about themselves. Gabriella didn't want to become inconsiderate like that. It wouldn't hurt, she told herself—it might even be good for her—to do as the fairies asked. The faster she finished the task they'd set for her, the faster they were likely to send her home. "Fine," she said again.

Except, of course, that Miss-mot thought the removal of her clothes was one big game. And the putting on of her new clothes was another game. Gabriella's nightgown would never look nor smell the same.

Parf stayed—in order to ridicule, not help.

And he continued not to be of help as Gabriella got the baby settled and put her down for a nap, and as he tagged along to the place where the laundry and laundry lines rested in the dirt. And all the while he offered words of unneeded advice so that Gabriella could hardly think for all his chattering.

Advice such as "There's the basket," as though Gabriella was incapable of seeing, and "Use your legs to lift," which people always seem to say when someone else is doing the lifting. He ended with "Don't fall" as Gabriella was scrambling down the stream bank to get to the water—as though anyone falls intentionally. She was just thinking, undiplomatically, what a useless boy he was, when she misstepped. (Gabriella was not the type of person to always point a finger in blame, but this may have had *something* to do with those fairy shoes pinching her toes.) She fell, sliding the rest of the way down the grassy incline and into the water, seat first.

Parf shook his head. "I said your feet was too big," he told her.

"So you did," she muttered. She wrung the hem of her gown to get at least some of the water out. There was little she could do about the mud and grass stains.

"You're lucky it's a warm day and the sun will dry you off soon enough."

"Yes, lucky," she said. "That's what I was just thinking."

Parf snorted, which showed he knew she'd said the opposite of what she meant. Muddy bottom or not, that was a diplomatic transgression on her part.

She needed to change the topic in order to smooth over her lapse in manners. "I'm surprised," Gabriella said—not criticizing, but trying to learn more—"that your mother doesn't use magic to launder your family's clothing."

Parf snorted again. "That just goes to show how much you know—or, rather, *don't know*—about magic. You can't just *wish* things."

"I didn't know," Gabriella explained mildly.

"Of course you didn't."

"I don't have any previous experience with fairies."

"Well, I don't have no previous experience with *people*," Parf countered, "but I don't go around thinking they can wish their laundry clean."

Gabriella wanted to point out that *of course* people couldn't wish their laundry clean, because people were not magical creatures. *People* had to make clothing that fit whoever was going to wear it, rather than conjuring items out of the local vegetation for an entire family. But while she was mentally trying out different ways to say this so that she didn't sound argumentative, Parf continued, "Present company excluded, obviously."

"I . . ." Gabriella shook her head. "I'm not following your meaning."

"Princesses."

"Ahmmm . . . That didn't clarify an awful lot."

"Princesses just wave a hand, and everyone jumps to do your bidding."

"That's not true." Argumentative or not, Gabriella had to set him straight. She repeated, "That's not true."

Parf shrugged. "I'm sure you know."

"Well, I do."

"Ever done the laundry before?"

"Well, no, but—"

"Ever make your own clothes?"

"People have different tasks—"

"Ever take care of younger brothers and sisters?"

"I don't have—"

"Yup," Parf said. "Princesses just have to say their wishes out loud. Sounds like princess magic to me."

Gabriella put her hands on her hips. "If that were true, I could wish myself back home."

"Too bad your magic don't work here."

If she didn't stop talking now, she would blurt out something unforgivable. She dumped the basket of fairy clothing into the water to begin washing.

Parf made a sound of contempt, and she was about to ask him what she'd done wrong now when she realized that two shirts and a dress were floating downstream. She captured them, but meanwhile a skirt floated by; reaching for that, she lost her footing and once again found herself sitting in the water.

By the time she'd retrieved all the clothing she could see— and she suspected she'd lost a few items to the current—Parf was sitting beneath a nearby tree, clapping as though she were putting on a show.

"If you'd helped me," she said, cramming the last dandelion headband into the basket, "I could be sure I caught everything."

"You didn't," Parf said. "And this way, I get to hear you explain all about it to Mumsy."

That was not something to which Gabriella was looking forward. "Am I finished?" Gabriella asked.

"Nooooo. You've dunked the clothes, not washed them."

Gabriella couldn't see any way but to come out and ask him. "How do I wash them?"

"You beat them against the rock to loosen the dirt." Parf pointed to where a round-topped rock poked out of the water.

The fairy clothes looked too delicate to withstand being beaten against a stone, and she did wonder if Parf was intentionally misleading her. Not that at this point she really cared.

But the fairy magic proved durable. The clothes didn't rip as Gabriella slammed them—and occasionally her fingers, which were not quite so durable—against the rock. She worked on one article of clothing at a time, so as not to lose any more. When she finished, she trudged back and forth from the rock, knee-deep in water, to the basket on dry land. No matter how mindful she tried to be, she tripped almost every time over the sodden skirt of her nightgown, as it grew longer from the weight of the water and mud it had soaked up.

And it wasn't just her nightgown that was causing her to trip. Her purple fairy shoes were beginning to look more and more like eggplants. No longer just because of the color, and not even due to their unfortunate shape. Vines were beginning to grow from them.

Parf, seeing her take note of this, pointed out: "You've overwatered the shoes. You'll have to trim them once we get back to the house."

Although she did her best to wring out the excess water from the fairy shirts, skirts, dresses, and breeches, the basket was still incredibly heavy as she hauled it up the bank. She could tell she hadn't done a thorough enough job, because water dripped out of the basket as she staggered back along the path to the fairies' home. Her shoes made rude squishing noises and continued to grow leafy. Parf didn't talk, but he did whistle, and that was almost as irritating. Would it be too much to expect a little help from him? Gabriella set the basket down and stretched, pressing her hands into her back. "Do you think maybe you might—"

"Nope," Parf cut her off. "Mumsy said *you*. Mumsy gets cranky when we don't follow her instructions."

Gabriella said, "I didn't see you worrying about her getting cranky when your brothers and sisters decided to cut the laundry lines."

Parf snorted. "Mumsy never said we couldn't cut the laundry lines."

"But—"

"Mumsy said *you* needed to do the laundry and fix the lines."

"But—"

"Mumsies know. They always know."

Gabriella sighed and picked up the basket, forgetting to use her knees. Her aching back reminded her.

At the hill, she restrung the lines. Her hands were stiff from all the washing and carrying, and the knuckles of her fingers were raw from repeated accidental smackings against the rock. In fact, Gabriella's arms, shoulders, legs, and back were *all* sore, and her hair kept falling into her face. She was almost willing to consider that the fairies' short, spiky hair might be an improvement. She grew light-headed from bending down over the basket, then standing up to clip the clothes to the lines. Or maybe it was from hunger. The sun was overhead, and she hadn't eaten since last night.

"They'll take forever to dry," Parf observed disapprovingly, "seeing as you haven't wrung them out sufficiently."

What Gabriella *wanted* to wring was Parf's neck. She had never had such a thought before, and was ashamed for it. But only a little.

She reminded herself that fairies usually exchanged babies for babies. She was only here as a game, one thought up by bored children. Now that she had spent the morning doing their bidding without fuss or drama, surely they would lose interest in her. Surely they would return her home.

In fact, just as she and Parf arrived at the house, the other children came running outside.

And continued right past Gabriella and Parf.

"You missed the midday meal!" they called, a moment before they disappeared into the surrounding woods.

So much for surely-they-would-return-her-home.

"Good thing I had a big breakfast," Parf told Gabriella. "You?"

"No." She forced her weary resentment not to show. "I woke up from a night's slumber, surrounded by you and your family, and have not yet had a chance to dine."

Parf considered this news. Gabriella hoped he might say that, if she explained what had happened, perhaps Mumsy would find a little leftover something for her to eat.

Of course, as far as explanations went, unless the fairies returned her home now, Gabriella would *also* have to explain to Mumsy about the lost clothing; she was not looking forward to that.

In any case, what Parf ended up saying was, "Well, then, you better be quick at the evening meal. The little ones tend to grab up anything good really quick."

Gabriella sighed. "That's nice to know." She didn't have the energy to say more.

Amanda, she thought. *Amanda will have seen that the fairy girl is not me. Amanda will have raised the alarm that I am gone, and that a change-ling has taken my place.*

She assumed her father or one of his advisers would know how to get to the fairy realm. She wished she had paid more attention during her geography lessons, because she had no idea whether the fairies even shared the same world as her own kingdom, or if it could only be reached through magical means.

But her father would know, or would find out.

How far off could rescue be?

PHLEG

Phleg and Ellen were walking in the castle, either using a different route back from the garden or heading toward a different room for the midday meal. Phleg would not put it beyond people to have a different room for each meal.

She was just thinking of how difficult people were when they went around a corner and almost collided with a tall, older man. He wore many gold buttons and had golden tassels on his shoulders. Clearly someone important—and someone who did not appreciate being almost collided with.

Ellen curtseyed and murmured, "Your Highness."

So this was the king. Apparently kings didn't walk around wearing crowns all the time, which surprised Phleg. If she'd been a king, she thought, she would never take her crown off. But, now that she thought about it, the queen hadn't been wearing hers at the breakfast meal, either.

Come to think of it, surely princesses had crowns, too. If Ellen had been a good servant, Phleg decided, she should have asked about that this morning, along with all the other questions about clothing: *So, Princess Gabriella, are you going to be wearing your crown today?* Phleg determined that she would send Ellen to fetch her crown during the midday meal, so that she could wear it that afternoon.

But meanwhile, Phleg wondered if princesses curtseyed to their fathers. She decided to bob her head, which might be taken for a curtsey if you were looking for one. "Hello, Daddy," she said.

"What?" the imposing man bellowed at her.

His hair was gray, so maybe he was old enough that he had become hard of hearing. But something about his tone made her suspect he was incredulous rather than unsure. And he was without a doubt displeased. Maybe princesses were more formal with their parents than fairies were. She gave a definite curtsey. She'd seen Ellen and other servants do it often enough that she had the general idea of how. She tottered off balance so that Ellen lunged—overdramatically, Phleg thought—to keep her from tipping over, and this time Phleg said, formally, "Hello, Father."

Still not right—she could tell by the way his brows came together, even before he thundered, "What ails the girl?"

She glanced at Ellen, who made an obvious concerted effort to close her mouth, which for some reason was hanging open. Ellen gathered herself, then said, "Princess Gabriella, this is King Leopold of Rosenmark, the father of Prince Frederic."

"Of course I know that," Phleg said. "That's what I meant to say: Hello, Fred's . . . um . . . daddy-father."

Clearly King Leopold was not persuaded that this was what Phleg had meant to say. "What is this?" Apparently, the man never spoke at a level short of a roar. "Are you addled in the head? What trickery is King Humphrey trying to get away with?"

"No trickery, sire," Ellen said. "Princess Gabriella struck her head this morning and is sometimes momentarily confused. Temporarily, I'm sure."

"And so she's been rolling in the dirt?" the king shouted.

Admittedly her dress was not quite as clean as when she'd put it on, and—all right!—there were one or two twigs snagged in the fabric from when she'd been in the garden, listening to Fred's story of the adventures of Telmund. *Rolling in the dirt* was a clear exaggeration, however. For the sake of making her feel bad.

"I have *not* been rolling in the dirt," Phleg protested. She heard Ellen's sharp intake of breath. *"What?"* Phleg snapped at the servant.

Ellen's eyes were wide and her face had gone white.

But it was Leopold who answered Phleg. His voice was loud enough that Phleg wouldn't have been surprised if it shook the tapestries off the walls. "How dare you! Nobody talks back to me that way! Not even another king! Much less a . . . grubby . . . snip of a princess from a third-rate kingdom who's lucky we're even *considering* aligning ourselves with you."

Phleg put her hands on her hips. "Oh yeah?" she said. Ellen yanked at the nearer of Phleg's arms in an attempt to get her attention—either that or to make her look less confrontational— but Phleg refused to take the warning. "Oh *yeah*?" she repeated, for the momentum it gave her. "Well, and *you* shouldn't talk to *me* that way, either."

A new voice spoke up: a calm, let's-be-reasonable voice that

Phleg recognized even before turning around to see that Fred was behind her. His younger brother, Telmund, hung back, apparently unsettled by all the shouting. "Come, come, Father," Fred said jovially. "I'm sure Princess Gabriella means no harm."

"No harm?" The king was so angry he was spitting, which Phleg suspected was probably as rude for people as it was for fairies. "King Humphrey is trying to pass off this addlepated shrew of a daughter as normal? As worthy of union with our family?"

"I'm sure this is all a misunderstanding," Fred told him. "Princess Gabriella was in the garden with me and Telmund; that's how she happens to have a few leaves caught in her skirts. There's no reason for you to bully—"

He stopped short in his explanation when Leopold sucked in a breath. "And is this why you refused to join the hunting party this morning? To defy me? To spend time, unchaperoned, with this . . . this . . . person?"

Fred repeated, "With me *and Telmund*."

"She's already a bad influence on the two of you!" Leopold's voice suddenly went quiet. Unexpectedly, that was worse than the shouting. The tiny hairs on the nape of Phleg's neck stood up as the king finished, "I will not tolerate this."

But if he meant to say anything further, he was interrupted by the arrival of another imposing older man, to whom Ellen bowed and murmured, "Your Highness."

Phleg was not going to risk being wrong again. She folded her arms over her chest and glowered.

The new man kissed her on the forehead, but then turned a fierce expression onto Leopold. "What's amiss?" he asked. "We could hear the commotion in the throne room."

"What's amiss?" Leopold's volume continued to be low and dangerous. "Your daughter is a simpleton. And unmannered on top of that."

"She is not, and she is not," King Humphrey stated. "How dare you—"

"I decree the wedding is off!"

Phleg gasped. "No," she squeaked.

"Father!" Fred cried.

"No insolence from you!" Leopold ordered his son.

"Of course the wedding is off," King Humphrey said, putting his arm protectively around Phleg. "We wouldn't have you."

"No," Phleg repeated. She was supposed to pass as the princess. She wasn't supposed to ruin the princess's wedding plans. And Fred seemed so nice.

But Leopold took her response the wrong way. He took her to mean that she, too, wouldn't have them. "Insufferable brat!"

"Father!" Fred repeated. "The betrothal is set. Surely if we all sit down—"

While Phleg's attention was on the two kings, Gabriella's mother had entered the corridor. The queen rested her hand on Phleg's shoulder, but spoke to her husband and to her formerly-meant-to-be-daughter's-husband's-father. (What *was* that relationship named? Brother-in-law, once removed?) In any case, the two men were standing toe-to-toe with each other, looking close to coming to blows.

"Perhaps if we all sit down," the queen began, "and have something cool to drink—"

"I will have nothing more to do with this conniving family," Leopold shouted.

"Leopold!"

All the males in the room—not just Leopold, but also Gabriella's father, and Fred, and his brother, as well as a couple of stray servants—*all* of them gave guilty starts. A woman Phleg hadn't seen before spoke in a commanding, condemning, surely-I-must-be-mistaken-because-I-could-not-have-just-heard-you-say-THAT tone of voice. This new woman stepped forward to stand beside the queen, matching exactly both the look and voice Mumsy used when Daddy had irritated her beyond bearing. No question about it: Leopold must be this woman's husband, making her Fred's mumsy.

Although he was clearly cowed by his wife, Leopold tried to explain. "That girl . . ." His finger shook as he pointed at Phleg. "That girl . . . There's something not right with her! Mark my words! She's no proper princess!"

Oh no! How had he guessed in so short a time? Once Leopold explained to his wife, she would take his side. Once that happened, Gabriella's parents would see the truth, too. Phleg couldn't stand the thought that Parf had been right: She hadn't been able to pass as a princess for three days. She hadn't even managed for half a day. Parf would never let her hear the end of it.

And even worse than that, if she lost the bet, she'd have to do his chores, on top of her own, for a week! No chance now to

61

wear that crown. No more comfy bed. No more all-she-could-eat meals. No more of Fred's stories.

There was nothing Phleg could think to say or do to fix the situation.

But she refused to go home this early, admitting defeat.

All she could think was that she needed to get out of there.

So she turned and ran.

∽ *Chapter 4* ∾

Could This Day Get Any Worse?

PRINCESS GABRIELLA

Gabriella realized she had no idea what fairies ate. Now that she thought about it, she found in the back of her mind a vague notion that they might sip nectar, like hummingbirds.

Though *sipping* seemed too delicate a word to associate with this particular family of fairies.

Especially once Parf led Gabriella into the kitchen.

To a certain extent, it looked more like a regular kitchen than Gabriella would have expected, with cupboards, counters, a dry sink, a vat for holding water, and both a fire for cooking over and an oven for baking.

But it was the filthiest kitchen she had ever seen. Granted, she had only ever seen the one in the castle, but *never* was that kitchen in such disarray, even after state dinners with many, many guests. The fairies' kitchen was covered with grimy handprints all over every surface—buttery, floury, milky, jammy, mustardy handprints—and enough used dishes and bowls and pots and pans that it almost seemed as though the fairies must have had a state dinner of their own.

Except that some of the piles of greasy dishes were dusty, *as well as* crusty, indicating they'd sat for a good long while. This was a wonder, as the stacks were piled very precariously. The dishes were all different sizes and shapes, having been fashioned from a variety of leaves. As with the fairies' clothing, magic had made the leaves bigger than they would have been in nature, and more durable. Some were spring green, some deep summer olive, and others showed autumn's riot of color. The cups and bowls looked to have started life as acorns and walnuts and mushroom caps; and the pots were hollowed-out gourds and melons.

Amid all this chaos, Mumsy sat with one of her legs stretched out on the table, painting her toenails and drinking tea—chamomile by the smell of it. Gabriella suspected the fairy mother routinely made more tableware when she ran out of clean leaves, rather than wash what she already had. She certainly was showing no inclination for tidying up now.

Despite all this, and much to her embarrassment, Gabriella's stomach grumbled.

"Kitchen's closed," Mumsy snarled without looking up from her toes. "I'm too busy to fix individual meals for children who can't bestir themselves to make it here at mealtime."

"But—" Gabriella started.

"No," Mumsy said.

It may well have been a breach of protocol to insist—but Gabriella was too weary to remember, and she continued as though Mumsy hadn't spoken. "I was busy working. Doing the laundry."

"No exceptions," Mumsy told her. "If I said yes to you, I'd have to say yes to all the other children, and then I'd be a slave to the kitchen." She looked at Gabriella and Parf coolly. "I'll not be a slave to the kitchen."

Parf shrugged. "I tried to tell her. But Gabby's stubborn."

"Well, then, you shouldn't have brought her in here."

Parf nodded, even though Mumsy was once again absorbed in her toenails and was no longer looking at him to see that he was agreeing with her. "She has something to tell you," Parf added.

Mumsy sighed. Either that, or she was blowing her toenails dry. "Something *besides that* she's inconsiderate and expects me to indulge her every whim and coddle her and jump up and make special meals for her on *her* schedule?"

Indulging? Coddling? Gabriella said, "I don't—"

"Yes, something else," Parf interrupted. "It's about the laundry."

Mumsy looked at Gabriella darkly.

Gabriella gulped. "I . . . may have lost a couple articles of clothing to the current in the river."

The ever-helpful Parf clarified, "That's *a couple* only by people-count, apparently. *We* would say *several*."

Mumsy flapped her wings in irritation, then swung her leg around to stand up, oblivious to the fact that she knocked her tea over in the process. The brown liquid pooled on the wood, then seeped to the edge and beyond. Drip. Drip. Drip. "You clumsy girl!" Mumsy shouted. "Humans are so careless with things! Magic doesn't come cheap, you know! Do you think it grows on trees? And, speaking of growing, look what you've done to your shoes! Shoes I made! Those were some of my best work!"

Gabriella looked. The purple monstrosities had begun to sprout pale mauve buds.

"Now I'll have to take inventory," Mumsy said, "and see what I need to replace. Do you think I'm here for your own personal convenience?"

"No, Mu . . ." It was one thing to think of the fairy as *Mumsy*. Gabriella couldn't bring herself to call her that—though she tried, several times, so that what she actually said was, "No, Mu-mu-muuum." Her words came out barely a whisper, and she didn't look up from the offending shoes.

Mumsy swept from the room, pausing only to snap from the doorway, "The least you can do is clean up the kitchen!"

The least I could do, Gabriella thought, *is to sit down on the floor and refuse to do anything.*

But, really, the floor was too sticky for her to consider that seriously.

Do what they want today, she told herself. Surely after one full day they would send her home.

"There's water in that vat," Parf told her. "You can heat it up in the cauldron that goes over the fire." (That one must have once been a pumpkin.) "Wash the dishes in that. But then, of course, you'll have to go fetch more water from the river to replace what you've used."

66

"Of course," Gabriella said. The poor people of her father's kingdom would have to do the same, and she was not the kind of princess who thought herself better than simple farmers and tradesmen.

Dish after dish she scraped and scoured. And pans—lots of greasy pans. And pots, some so big she practically had to crawl inside to chip away at the dried food accumulated at the bottom so that bits ended up stuck to her and her dress.

Parf picked a leaf of limp kale from her hair. "I'm guessing you ain't so upset about missing the midday meal that you're saving this to eat later."

"Maybe," Gabriella said, not quite sure if she was joking.

Parf snorted and tossed the leaf into the bucket of wash water before she could make up her mind.

Just about every dish had been used and the cupboards were all but bare. Gabriella couldn't stand to put clean dishes on dirty shelves, so she wiped down the shelves—and the doors. And mopped the floor. And went to the river—twice—with a bucket to refill the vat.

In between all that, she had to take down the finally-dry laundry from the line, then fold the basketful of clothing and put it away in the closet using a system of organization that— if Parf wasn't making it up on the spot—never became apparent to her.

She was staggering from fatigue by the time she made it back to the kitchen from her second trip to the river.

Parf took the bucket from her to empty it into the vat, the first help he'd been all day.

Gabriella was so surprised that she momentarily wondered if Mumsy had come back into the room. Parf might want Mumsy to think he'd worked all afternoon, too.

But they were alone.

"Here," Parf said sourly. At first she was too tired to even focus on what he held. It was a peach, golden pink and just soft enough to show it was perfectly ripe.

Was this some sort of trick? Gabriella knew there were legends where humans were trapped in a magical realm by eating something—but her teachers had told her this wasn't true. It was just the way overprotective mothers tried to discourage their children from accepting food from strangers. Gabriella was too tired and hungry to try to work out Parf's motive, beyond that it was a momentary lapse into kindness. "Thank you," she said, her voice coming soft and shaky—maybe from weariness, maybe from gratitude.

He grunted. "Yeah, well, don't get used to it. And don't tell Mumsy."

"Certainly not," Gabriella agreed, even though it was bad manners to speak with one's mouth full. The peach was juicy and tasty and wonderful.

Perfectly timed—perfectly badly timed—Mumsy chose then to walk into the kitchen. "Don't tell Mumsy what?"

Parf looked at the ceiling as though he had come to inspect the architecture.

Gabriella hid the remainder of the peach behind her back and swallowed what she'd already bitten off, hoping there was no juice on her chin.

If nothing else, Mumsy knew children—be they her own or someone else's. She twirled her finger, a gesture for Gabriella to turn around. Parf wasn't standing close enough for her to try to hand off the evidence to him. Besides, it had been so long since she'd eaten, she couldn't bear to give up this tiny meal after only one bite. Gabriella brought her hand out from behind her back, wondering if she could stuff the whole rest of the peach into her mouth before Mumsy took it away from her.

But Mumsy only shrugged. She cooed at Parf, "Well, isn't that sweet?"

Parf's glowering face and stiffened spine showed very clearly that he did not appreciate being called *sweet*.

Mumsy continued as though he hadn't reacted. "If you see fit to feed her, that's your business." To Gabriella she said, "And if that ruins your appetite and you don't want your evening meal, but then you get hungry later, it's Parf you can go to for meals between meals."

Gabriella doubted any one peach—as scrumptious as it might be—could do more than take the edge off her hunger.

Mumsy looked around the kitchen and grunted, which Gabriella supposed was her understated way of saying *Good job*. What she did say was, "You can help me get the evening meal prepared and on the table."

Parf took that as his cue to make himself scarce. Either that, or he was still stinging from Mumsy having called him *sweet*.

Preparing a meal was another of those tasks Gabriella had never done or spent much time wondering about.

69

"Fetch the cucumber plate," Mumsy would say, and Gabriella didn't know if that was a plate to hold cucumbers or one that had been made from a cucumber. In either case—even though she had surely just put the plate into the cupboard minutes ago— she had to ask, "Where is it? What does it look like?" And, "How much salt is a pinch of salt?" And, "How much of the onion do I peel away? Just the papery part, or the first layer after that? Is there a center that can't be eaten? How *thin* are 'thin' slices?"

Mumsy called her hopeless after every question. "If you're trying to get out of helping by acting useless," she warned, "it won't work."

"I just want to do it right," Gabriella said.

Mumsy snorted but told her, "What you've got is not done half badly."

Apparently the biggest meal of the day was at midday. This was a smaller one, with various fruits and vegetables that Mumsy did appear to have a knack for fixing and presenting. No meat, Gabriella noted, but she wasn't sure if that was coincidence or due to a conscious choice for this meal. Or if it was just the fairies' way.

Next was trying to corral the children—Mumsy made more of an effort to get everyone to the table than Gabriella would have expected from her attitude earlier—and to get hands and faces at least somewhat clean.

"Is Daddy coming tonight?" one of the children asked.

"Not that he's let me know of," Mumsy said. "No-account sluggard."

Gabriella was curious but didn't want to be nosy, so she didn't ask about the children's father.

And then they started eating. It was—as Parf had indicated—a bit of chaos. Children reached over one another, grabbing food from bowls (and occasionally from one another's plates) with their bare hands. There was kicking beneath the table, elbows atop the table, and conversations with mouths full of food. Despite all this, Gabriella found the meal was unexpectedly delicious, and she didn't think this was just because she was hungrier than she had ever been before. "This is *so* good," she told Mumsy—several times.

Mumsy grunted the first time, didn't answer at all the second, looked suspicious the third, but after the fourth she announced to no one in particular, "It's nice to have someone appreciate your efforts."

The children—except for Parf, who was still sullen—were eager to please, and they too started chanting, "It's good, Mumsy."

Mumsy's face softened for the first time that day.

Which did not mean that *she* softened. "It's your job to clean up," she told Gabriella, once the meal was finished.

"Ah," Gabriella said. "Because I'm taking Phleg's place, and that's one of Phleg's duties."

Though kitchen cleanup had clearly not happened in a much longer time than Phleg had been away, Mumsy just looked at Gabriella levelly and said, "Yes." Then she said, "Children, off to bed. We have an early day tomorrow."

"We have an early day every day," Parf groused.

71

"Gabby didn't," several of the others said. "She slept halfway through the morning."

"Well, we can't all be princesses," Mumsy said, shooing the children out of the kitchen, "with our own personal helpers."

Gabriella thought Mumsy was referring to the castle servants, but Parf's face reddened, and Gabriella realized Mumsy meant him. Not that he'd been any help, but he *had* hung around all day.

Unfortunately, the children realized the same thing. Gabriella could hear their tinny voices chanting from their bedchamber: "Parf's got a girlfriend! Parf's got a girlfriend!"

And Parf protesting, "Do not!"

Parf? How could any of the children think that, when he clearly despised everything about her?

Well, but he *had* given her that peach.

Still . . .

Parf? Gabriella thought. *PARF?* That was . . . unbelievable . . . disgusting . . . Well, maybe not *disgusting*, but unsettling. She wasn't sure how she felt about that possibility. She wasn't even sure how she felt about being betrothed to Prince Frederic, and she'd known since she was seven that she was to marry him.

Prince Frederic! Gabriella had forgotten all about him. He and his parents had arrived from Rosenmark yesterday for the official coming-of-age betrothal ceremony. She had seen him briefly at supper the night before. He certainly didn't know her well enough that he would realize a fairy had been substituted for her, any more than she . . .

72

No, she told herself, picturing Parf substituting himself for Prince Frederic. She *would* notice such an exchange.

Gabriella sighed at the state of the kitchen she had spent so long cleaning. How could it have gotten so messy again so quickly? She mopped the splattered lingonberry relish off the floor and walls. Swept up bread crumbs. Washed the dishes and put them away.

By the time she was finished, the sounds of everyone else settling down for the night had quieted, and the fairy house was silent.

She could run away.

If she had any idea where she was.

But running away now would just further complicate things. A full day—dawn to dawn—was such a round, even amount of time. The kind of limit that fairy children would give to the duration of a spell.

I'm going to wake up in my own bed, she told herself. Three times, she told herself, as a charm.

It wasn't that late, wasn't even all that dark, given that the walls glowed gently. But once she was finished with her tasks, and now that her hunger had been satisfied, it was replaced by exhaustion. Gabriella staggered into the children's bedchamber and to the pile of straw on which she had awoken what felt to be *days* ago.

Tomorrow I have to get fresh straw, she thought—but then immediately caught herself. Tomorrow morning she would wake up on clean satin sheets that someone *else* had washed and hung to dry. And pressed. She felt fortunate that the magically made fairy clothing did not need pressing. Just the occasional trimming.

73

Gabriella had kicked off her eggplant shoes during the preparation of the meal. Now she saw that someone had brought them in and set them by her bed. The vines and buds had been cut back for her.

Parf?

Judging by the soft snores, both from the boys' side of the room and the girls', everyone was asleep already. Miss-mot and the next-youngest girl were on Gabriella's straw, and she had to rearrange their arms and legs to give herself enough room. Which was no reason to feel sorry for herself. *Princesses don't cry just because they're tired and miss their parents,* she told herself. The only reason her eyes were scratchy was because of the straw. Even so, once Gabriella was lying down, the next-youngest one shifted to snuggle against her.

"Good night," the child mumbled sleepily.

"Good night," Gabriella answered, though she suspected the girl mistook her for her sister Phleg. It gave her a nice feeling, while at the same time it made her eyes feel even more scratchy from the straw.

Still, she was sure—sure!—that tomorrow she would be home and everything would be back to normal.

PHLEG

Phleg ran.

People were running after her, calling for her to stop, come back, she didn't have to marry Prince Frederic if she didn't want to—or she *could*, if *that* was what she wanted—somehow they'd fix everything and work things out with his awful father.

Obviously, King Leopold was not one of the chasers assuring her of this.

On the other hand, his wife—she of the big voice—was.

And so was her father—no! Princess Gabriella's father. *Stop thinking of him as YOUR daddy*, Phleg commanded herself. But it was sweet how long King Humphrey followed the girl he believed was his daughter. Who'd have guessed such an old man could run so fast?

Her mother—*Gabriella's* mother—barely made it out of the castle. Phleg heard the commotion when the queen tripped over her long skirts and fell, and the other queen and several of the servants stopped their pursuit of the runaway princess in order to attend to her. Phleg also stopped, turning her head at the cry of dismay from the onlookers. Gabriella's mother motioned for the pursuers to keep going.

That's what comes from too many undergarments, thought Phleg, who had hoisted her own gown and flouncy underskirts above her knees to prevent just such a mishap. She hoped the queen wasn't hurt. Phleg's coming here was supposed to be for *fun*— admittedly fun for Phleg, not necessarily for Princess Gabriella or her family—but it wasn't fun for anybody to break up betrothals and injure parents.

Phleg was far enough ahead that she could spare a moment to watch.

Torn between helping wife or daughter, King Humphrey wavered a moment after he realized what had happened behind him. A cluster of servants had been running close on his heels. (They had been holding back out of respect for their king, in order not to outdistance him.) Now that he'd faltered, they surged past and quickly closed the gap on the hesitating Phleg.

The queen again waved her hand dismissively—which Phleg took as evidence she was not seriously hurt, and which King Humphrey took as permission to leave his wife to the care of the servants. He once more took up the chase, but it was clear the servants who were ahead of him were superior runners.

Phleg, too, resumed running, putting on a burst of speed of her own.

Past the flower garden and the kitchen garden she ran, past the stables and the blacksmith and the tradesmen's shops. The servants weren't catching up to her, but she wasn't pulling any farther ahead. She could see the wall that surrounded the castle precincts, and headed toward that.

The servants began yelling and waving their arms at the castle guards. There were two of them, positioned by the draw-bridge that allowed access to and from the castle over the moat. It took the soldiers a few moments of gawping at the approaching mass of runners, led so improbably by their princess, before they finally caught on. They began turning the winch wheel that would raise the bridge—and block her in.

Phleg kicked off her blue brocade slippers—she often went without shoes at home—to give herself better traction as the bridge began to angle up, up: a steeper incline with every thud of her bare feet across the wood. The guards hesitated. This was, after all, the princess. They must have doubted themselves, thinking that surely they were not being asked to prevent their princess from leaving the castle if that's what she wanted—and that gave her just enough time to get to the end of the drawbridge before the slope became too steep to climb. Then she threw herself into the air, off the drawbridge and in the direction of the farther shore.

Oh yeah, she thought, about one heartbeat too late, *no wings.*

Her fairy wings, puny as they were, would not only have slowed her descent but would also have given her some control over direction. But they had been enchanted away along with her face, her spiky silver-white hair, and her much more reasonable height.

Fortunately, her momentum wasn't enough to carry her to the hard, gravelly roadway on the far side. Instead, she landed in the moat with a spectacular splash that knocked the breath out of her.

She came up sputtering, algae draped over her head like green, dripping locks, just in time to hear the drawbridge thump flush with the castle wall.

So much for those chasing her.

For the moment.

Her layers of clothes weighed her down, but Phleg managed to paddle to the shore and hoisted herself up onto the grassy bank.

Behind her, she could hear the creaking and groaning of wood and rope as the guards worked to once again lower the bridge. She had to get moving fast, so she sprinted across the grass and onto the road.

"Ouch, ouch, ouch!" The people-road was harder and more uneven than the forest floor. And princess feet were more delicate than fairy feet. If she stopped now and let her pursuers catch up, she guessed that the servants would probably carry her back to spare those fragile feet of hers—well, Gabriella's. And the king and queen would assure her that everything would be all right. But everything wasn't all right. The other king, Fred's father, had taken an instant dislike to her. Not only that, he'd guessed that she was an imposter. He'd come right out and shouted it to everyone: "She's no proper princess!"

He would convince his wife, and she would convince their sons. *Everyone* would side with him. There was nothing Phleg could do about that. Probably Princess Gabriella could smooth things over. Well . . . maybe. Phleg hoped so. Once Phleg returned her to the castle. But as for Phleg, she wasn't going to give Parf and her other siblings the satisfaction of seeing her fail. And they would know she had failed if she reversed the spell that made her look like Gabriella, for that would make them change places. Gabriella, whatever she was doing back home, wherever she was, would disappear, replaced by Phleg.

Couldn't even last one day, her brothers and sisters would taunt her. All of them. Though especially Parf.

But . . .

The road skirted the edge of the forest, a boundary separating the forest from the castle with its surrounding cultivated fields—the humans' domain. Phleg made it across the road and ran into the woods. Her brothers and sisters wouldn't know she had failed if she held on to the princess's form here in the forest. They would assume she had spent the time that she'd looked like the princess—all three days of it—in the castle. Phleg felt she had experienced enough just in this little time impersonating Gabriella that she could make up accounts of how she had spent the remaining two days. After all, she had a good imagination.

Running in the forest is something all fairies are used to. Phleg knew everything there was to know about the forest, and this made it easy for her to elude those who were pursuing her. For a while she could hear them calling out to her, begging her to please show herself, to come home, to spare her parents. Then, as the search party grew weary, their voices faded, but she could still hear them, more and more distantly, stomping about with their great big feet, breaking through the brush because they were too tall, too broad, and too clumsy to go under or between.

And then, finally, she couldn't hear them at all.

Phleg ran a bit more, wading through streams, climbing trees, and jumping to the near-enough branches of other trees, until she was sure they'd never be able to find her. People, even hunters, weren't that good in the forest.

She was sad to have left behind all that good food, but *really* she'd had more for breakfast than she usually did all day, and she knew perfectly well how to find fruits and nuts and berries when she did get hungry again tomorrow. She was also sad to leave behind that big, soft bed that didn't need to be shared with any little sisters. But grass and leaves would make comfortable bedding, and fairies frequently sleep outdoors in the summer. The beautiful princess gown she'd chosen this morning—well, that Ellen had chosen for her—was torn and stained beyond repair. It would be sad not to get to choose another one.

And Phleg never *had* gotten to wear a crown.

But—and here was a good thing—there was no one in the forest to tell her she needed to wear a scratchy underskirt. With this happy thought, Phleg wriggled out of that particular item of clothing and tossed it over her shoulder and into the stream she had just crossed.

"Good-bye, scratchy undergarment," she called as the current carried it away. "You were good for poofing out my dress, but that was your only redeeming feature."

She had run long enough that her hair—algae and all—had dried. So had her dress.

Phleg yawned. When she caught glimpses of the sky, it was beginning to turn pink and orange from the sunset. So . . . almost-but-not-quite evening. Not so very late. Still, she decided that it was time to bed down for the night.

Since fairies are friends to all the creatures who live in the forest, there was nothing to fear from them. It wasn't worry that unexpectedly kept her awake after she laid her head down on a huge, squishy mushroom cap, or lack of comfort. After a while, she realized she wasn't used to the quiet. No brothers or sisters meant no chatter.

Not that she missed them.

I like the quiet, Phleg thought. *I'm just not used to it.*

"Hmph!" she said out loud. And she invited a rabbit that was hopping past to lie down next to her—not because she was lonely, but because the rabbit looked tired.

Petting the rabbit's soft fur wasn't enough to distract herself from the silence. The only sounds she could hear were the regular rustlings and gurglings of a healthy forest at night. So she thought back on the story she'd heard Fred making up for his little brother. It had been a good story. Phleg began from the beginning—well, the beginning that she had heard—and mentally went over the details.

She hadn't spied Fred in the crowd of servants and royalty chasing her, and she hadn't heard him; she would have been able to pick his voice out from the clamor of the others. It wasn't that she felt disappointed—it would have been silly to feel disappointed—she just . . . had noticed not noticing him. Fred's father had probably ordered the boys and their mother to start packing their bags for home before she even made it out of the moat.

Fred had stood up to his father for her—well, for Princess Gabriella—and that had been nice of him. Phleg guessed that the real princess wouldn't have properly appreciated what Fred had tried to do, because princesses were used to things like that. Phleg wondered if the real princess would have enjoyed Fred's stories. Phleg hadn't meant to ruin things between them. Of course, she hadn't meant to ruin things for herself, either.

"Want to hear a story?" she asked the rabbit, just in case he was missing his family.

It wasn't that she missed hers; it wasn't that she was practicing for when she could share Fred's story with her brothers and sisters. Because she didn't like them well enough to do anything like that . . .

✐ *Chapter 5* ✐

Second Day, No Better Than the First

PRINCESS GABRIELLA
✦❧❧❧✦

This time, when the fairy children began to stir in the morning, Gabriella heard them and began to wake up.

She told herself, *The servants are being awfully noisy this morning.*

She told herself, *My goodness, what a strange dream I had!*

She told herself, *I must have tossed and turned all night—that's why I'm tired and sore even after a good night's sleep in my big, soft, comfortable bed.*

She told herself, *Don't open your eyes.*

Miss-mot squealed and threw herself onto Gabriella as though Gabriella were a pillow.

Gabriella opened her eyes, saw where she was, and began to cry.

Miss-mot decided to join in, sobbing and hiccuping.

One of the slightly older sisters picked up Miss-mot and asked, "Did she hurt you?"

Gabriella was too upset to protest that no princess would ever hurt a child.

But then she saw that the older fairy girl held the squalling toddler tucked under her arm, disregarding the child's noise, not to mention the flailing arms and legs. Her violet eyes were looking at Gabriella. "Sometimes she falls into me like that, and I swear it feels like her arm must've gone right through me, and I expect when she gets up she's gonna have ahold of my spleen."

Switching from crying to laughing, Gabriella snorted—the most unprincessly sound she had ever made. "She just knocked the wind out of me," she explained, dabbing at her eyes with the sleeve of her nightgown.

"Then why you crying?"

It would be downright rude to say, *Because I don't want to be here.* So Gabriella said, "I guess I'm a bit homesick."

"You miss your mumsy?"

Before Gabriella could answer, Parf called from the boys' side of the room, where he was running his fingers through the hair of one of his brothers, trying—intentionally *trying*, Gabriella saw—to get it to stand up straight. "She misses her servants bowing and going, 'Yes, my lady. Of course, my lady. Your wish is my command, my lady.'"

"Nobody talks that way to me," Gabriella said.

"Bet they do," Parf scoffed.

"Bet they don't," Gabriella countered.

"Then what *do* you miss?" asked the girl who was holding Miss-mot. Miss-mot had stopped crying but was now squirming. The girl set her down.

84

"I do miss my mother," Gabriella admitted. "And my father. And my friends."

"And your brothers and sisters?" one of the boys asked.

"I don't have any of those," Gabriella said.

"None?" several of the fairy children asked in awed disbelief, as though she had said she had no fingers or lungs.

"Yeah, well," Parf said, "and she don't have no chores, neither. All she has to do is sit around and look pretty."

Parf saw his mistake as soon as two of his brothers started chanting, "Parf thinks the princess looks pretty, Parf thinks the princess looks pretty."

Which caused the girls to say, "She *is* pretty." Though a moment later, they qualified this statement, adding, one by one:

"Even if her hair is funny."

"And she doesn't have wings."

"And her eyes are a spooky color."

"And she's tall as a bear."

"I do have chores," Gabriella said, before they could think up anything else that was wrong with her appearance. "I need to make visitors to the palace feel welcome. In times of trouble, I need to always stay calm and happy so people don't worry. I need to be pleasant to everybody."

Parf snorted; Gabriella suspected he *often* made that sound. "Oh, that sounds like backbreakingly hard work," he scoffed.

Gabriella couldn't help herself. She said: "Yes, I've seen how easy it's been for *you* to make *me* feel welcome."

Parf snorted again, but had no other answer.

85

From down the hall, Mumsy hollered, "Is anybody coming to breakfast, or are you all going to stay in bed the whole day long? I swear, nobody appreciates all the work I do around here."

The fairy children continued to dawdle and poke one another and chatter among themselves.

Gabriella considered her situation. If leaving here was not going to be as easy as she had first thought, she realized, then she must fit in.

Well, perhaps not *fit in*.

She resolved: *I'm going to make the situation better by being the princess I'm meant to be.*

Looking at the fairy girl who had expressed concern for Gabriella's spleen, Gabriella raised her eyebrows and made a go-ahead-and-say-it gesture.

The girl's brows furrowed in concentration as she tried to figure out what Gabriella was indicating.

Gabriella mouthed the words she wanted the girl to say.

Unsurely, the girl said almost, though not quite, a question: "I do." Gabriella nodded, and the girl repeated it more confidently: "I do." Then, all at once, she understood and shouted it for Mumsy to hear: "I do appreciate all your work, Mumsy!"

Shouting from other rooms is common and discourteous, but Gabriella felt that, for this family, it was excusable.

"Well then, come and eat," Mumsy said, the pleasure evident in her voice, "before I feed it to the squirrels."

Their feet as noisy as a herd of panicked sheep, the children hurried to the kitchen, knocking into one another as they all tried to fit through the doorway more or less at once.

Gabriella followed, still wearing her mud-and-grass-stained and slightly crusty nightgown, then sat in the same chair she had the night before, not sure if everyone was assigned a seat or if that was too much order to expect.

Meanwhile, the fairy children crowded around the table, jostling one another, leaning over to reach their hands into the bowl that was set down in the middle, loading their plates with the pancakes Mumsy had made.

"My! This smells good!" Gabriella said. Pecan and cinnamon, by the scent of them. Watching the quickly dwindling stack, Gabriella hoped there would be some left by the time the bowl came round to her.

"This *tastes* good," Parf corrected her, already sitting down with his mouth full. Gabriella suspected—a very ungenerous suspicion—that his main purpose in proclaiming this was to gloat that he'd gotten his serving while she still sat and waited.

Mumsy had taken her share before even calling the children— which wasn't model maternal behavior—but she took Parf's compliment at face value. "Thank you," she said.

"It's very good," one of the other children chimed in.

"I like it, too," another, not to be outdone, said.

A couple more joined in, one to say, "The pancakes and the syrup are both yummy," and the other, "Pecans are my favorite."

"Well, I'm glad," Mumsy murmured, sounding almost bashful for all the praise.

Once the children had grabbed all the pancakes they wanted and had sat down, Gabriella said, "Parf, could you please pass the bowl?"

"Your arm broke?" he asked. "You want me to set some cakes on your plate for you and cut them up into small pieces and feed you?"

Gabriella only smiled as warmly as she could.

The boy next to Parf picked up the bowl and stretched across the table to hand it to Gabriella. Parf reached in for another helping. Which left one pancake for Gabriella.

"It *is* as good as it smells," Gabriella announced.

"It's even better with the syrup." One of the girls passed the smaller of two pitchers around several of her sisters to Gabriella. "I helped gather the maple sap last autumn."

"Then I definitely need to try it," Gabriella told her.

"And have some milk," a small boy said, picking up the second pitcher. He walked around to where Gabriella sat, three places down from him. "I milked Tansy myself."

"Why, thank you," Gabriella said. She sipped the milk, which had a stronger taste than the cow's milk she was used to. "Tansy is your goat?" she guessed.

This got yet another snort from Parf. "Not *our* goat," he said. "Only *people* hold other creatures captive. Tansy is *a* goat. One of several who sometimes visit and let us milk them in return for brushing or for treats. Sometimes we have sheep's milk, and we don't imprison them, neither."

As though Parf hadn't spoken, Gabriella nodded to the boy who had done the milking and said, "That's kind of Tansy, and kind of you." She drank the last of the milk faster than was strictly speaking proper, because she saw some of the children had finished their meals and were beginning to get up from the table. She asked Mumsy, "Shall each of us bring our own dishes to the sink and wash them, so that they don't gather in a big pile for you?"

"Or for you," Parf snickered.

Mumsy ignored him and said, "That would be nice."

Gabriella stood by the sink and helped the children. She was actually doing the majority of the work, but at least the children were trying. Some looked less eager to participate than others; a couple even grumbled. But only Parf flatly refused to cooperate, leaving his plate and cup on the table when he headed for the door.

"Oooh," one of the girls called after him—a girl who, if Gabriella had heard properly during breakfast, seemed to be called Lazy. "Guess he's shown *he's* the princess who expects to be waited on. Yes, Your Highness. Your wish is our command, Your Highness. Please let everybody else do for you, Your Highness."

Parf whirled around, but seeing all his siblings laughing at him, couldn't come up with anything better than, "Oh yeah, Lazy?"

"Yeah," Lazy and several others answered.

And Parf skulked away.

Mumsy came to the sink last and said, "I'll finish up." She waved her fingers in a dismissive gesture. "Go on, get out of here," she ordered the children, "before I find tasks for all of you."

The little ones were gone before she finished gesturing.

Which left only Gabriella and the next oldest girl, the one who had called Parf a princess and whose name may or may not have been Lazy. She looked to be maybe twelve or thirteen years old. She told Gabriella, "I'll be helping you and Parf today."

"Oh," Gabriella said, following the girl. "Parf again?" And to think that just yesterday she had speculated that he might like her. Clearly the opposite was true. She didn't know which was worse. "Are we doing more laundry?"

"No," the girl laughed. "You got us *all* caught up yesterday, even the winter clothes, whichen we won't be needing for another five months. Phleg and Parf normally take care of the animals in the morning. I get to help today because everyone figures you'll be useless."

Charming.

Remembering that Parf had rather clearly indicated that the fairies did not keep animals, Gabriella asked, "Which animals?"

Again Lazy laughed, but not unkindly. "Whichever come."

"All right," Gabriella said. "And, excuse me, this is terrible of me, and I really apologize, but I don't believe we were ever introduced. What's your name?"

"Daisy," the girl said.

Finally a normal name. Not that Gabriella knew any girls named Daisy, but it seemed like a name a nice tradesman's daughter or farmer's wife might have.

Before Gabriella could say anything, Daisy finished, "'cepting Parf and them, they call me Lazy. Or Crazy. Or Hazy. Not on account of that I *am* any of those things, but the rhyme is just too good not to use."

"I will not," Gabriella assured her. She stopped walking, inclined her head formally, and said, "I am honored to meet you, Daisy."

Daisy giggled and imitated Gabriella's action and tone. "Likewise, I'm sure, Gabby."

And Gabriella didn't even wince.

Outside, Parf was waiting for them. "Took your time," he grumbled.

"Only because we stayed to help," Daisy pointed out, "not like some idle loaf-abouts who couldn't get out of the kitchen fast enough."

It was a rude thing to say, and Gabriella was appreciative that Daisy was there to say it.

Shrugging, Parf turned his back on them, as if he was too big-of-spirit to engage in verbal squabbles, though Gabriella suspected he more likely didn't have a good comeback.

There were two logs lying lengthwise in the yard, and Parf sat on one of them, Daisy on the other. Gabriella sat next to Daisy.

"Become fast friends, have you?" Parf commented. "Lazy Daisy and Princess Gabby?"

"Oh, cleverly said," Gabriella acknowledged, trying to keep peace with Parf, since it appeared she was going to be spending more time with the family than she would have hoped. "Nice wordplay."

Daisy, who was younger, looked confused. But, on the other hand, so did Parf.

"What?" Daisy asked.

"Ahm . . ." Gabriella explained for Daisy's benefit, though she became increasingly suspicious that she was explaining to Parf also. "By saying *fast*, Parf could mean both that we became friends quickly, or that our friendship is firm. It's a witticism—a pun."

"Usually," Daisy told Gabriella, "Parf's puns are more like his name: barf with pee."

"Usually," Parf retorted, "there's no one around who can *get* my more complicated witty-sisms."

Gabriella didn't correct his pronunciation. "Look," she said, her voice a whisper, "a baby deer."

It wasn't exactly a baby—its spots were beginning to fade—but it was very young. It approached the clearing hesitantly.

"Oh, you bad, bad thing," Daisy chided, but in a gentle voice. "Did you leave the safe spot where your mumsy set you down, and now you've gotten lost?" She held her hands out, inviting the fawn closer. "That's all right. Stay with us. We'll watch over you. And your mumsy will know to come looking for you here."

The little deer approached Daisy as though it could understand, then folded its long, spindly legs beneath itself and lay down in front of the log where she sat. Where Gabriella sat, too. Gabriella held her breath at the wonder of it, never having been this close to a wild animal before. Daisy leaned down and petted its head.

Gabriella was close enough that she could see the creature's nostrils quiver. Such a soft, velvety nose . . .

Perhaps Daisy could tell what she was wanting but afraid to do. She took Gabriella's hand and placed it atop the little deer's head, so Gabriella could pet it. There were cushions at home made of deer hide, but touching a living deer was totally different.

"Here comes a wolf," Parf said quietly.

He said it so mildly and matter-of-factly that Gabriella *knew* he was making something up just to scare her.

Until she looked up and saw the gray-and-silver wolf approaching.

She yanked her hand back from the wonderfulness of petting a live deer and jumped to her feet, ready to run.

"Take it easy, princess," Parf said in the same low-key voice.

"He won't hurt you," Daisy added.

"Wolves never go after fairies," Parf said. "And only rarely do they attack humans. Only if the person is hurt, or the wolf is starving."

"Or if the wolf is hurt." Gabriella's voice shook, for she saw that the wolf was limping. Everyone knows that injured animals are dangerous because they can lash out.

"He knows we're here to help," Parf said.

"And he won't hurt the deer, either," Daisy said. "This is a place of sanctuary."

Indeed, the deer appeared perfectly at ease, lying at Daisy's feet. But that, Gabriella told herself, could be because its instincts warned it to be still so that it might be overlooked. This was a tactic that sometimes worked for young animals, and sometimes didn't.

Parf called to the wolf, the way Daisy had called to the deer. "Come on, big guy," he urged. "We can help."

The wolf—it was bigger than the biggest dog Gabriella had ever seen—sat down in front of Parf and held its paw up, as though to let Parf take a look. Even from where she sat, Gabriella could see part of a stick poking out of the flesh between the pads of the wolf's foot. The poor creature had stepped on the pointy end, she realized, which penetrated deep into the flesh. The wolf had chewed off part of the stick but hadn't been able to pull it out.

Parf spoke reassuringly and the wolf looked directly at him, as though understanding every word. Finally, Parf took hold of the ragged end of the stick and pulled. The wolf whimpered, but made no move as though to lunge or bite.

"There, all gone," Parf said. "You'll be better in no time. Gabby, you going to sit there like a great lump, or do you want to help?"

"Of course I want to help," Gabriella said, though she was less sure than she made herself sound. What if she did something wrong—something that would hurt the wolf, or would encourage it to hurt her?

Parf said, "Get the cocklebur leaves out of the bag beside me."

Gabriella hadn't even noticed before that Parf had brought a satchel outside with him. Slowly, she stood, aware that the wolf's amber-eyed gaze followed every move she made as she crossed over to where Parf and the satchel sat. It was full of all sorts of packets of ointments and leaves, fresh and dried. *Burrs* Gabriella would have been perfectly capable of recognizing. But cocklebur *leaves?*

"Ahmm . . . ," she said, her hand hovering over several that might have been.

But which apparently weren't.

"Nope," Parf said. "Nope. Nope. Keep moving. That one. Don't you know nothing?"

"Apparently not," Gabriella said. The leaf was triangular and felt a bit rough.

"Rub the leaf on the wound—it'll help stop the bleeding."

"Me?" Gabriella gulped. Fetching it was one thing. Handing it to Parf to use was all well and good. But tending the wolf herself? She held the leaf in her hand and looked at the wolf. "So . . . ," she asked Parf, ". . . this doesn't sting, does it?"

"Of course, it stings like crazy. We'll use the comfrey for his pain afterwards."

After what? Gabriella thought. *After the wolf bites off my hand?*

The wolf gave a throaty growl as her hand hovered over his paw.

"Just do it," Parf said. "You're making him nervous."

The last thing Gabriella wanted was a nervous wolf. She touched the leaf to his paw and he yelped. Gabriella recoiled.

"Speak sweetly to him," Daisy recommended.

Gabriella took a deep breath. "I just want to help," she assured the wolf. "I'm new to this, but Parf and Daisy are helping me to help you. They'll see to it that I'll help you get better." Had anybody ever used the word *help* so often?

Finally the wound stopped bleeding, stopped oozing, and then Parf gave her the go-ahead to use the comfrey.

After that, Daisy wrapped the paw with a bit of cloth that may have started life as an ivy vine. "Well done, Gabby!" she said.

95

The wolf lay down, resting his muzzle on his paws for a nap after all that tension.

"Not half bad," Parf corrected his sister.

And that was how they spent the morning, tending to animals that seemed to know to come to the fairies' house for help: a fox who'd had a run-in with a porcupine, a weasel with an eye infection, a stoat who was having trouble delivering her babies, animals with cuts or who had eaten something they shouldn't, or who—in some cases—just seemed to want attention, affection, and reassurance. Parf—though he continued to chide Gabriella as a know-nothing and to call his sister both Lazy *and* Crazy— was incredibly patient and gentle with the animals.

"Why do you do this?" Gabriella asked the fairy children.

"It's what fairies do," Daisy said.

Eventually Mumsy came home; Gabriella hadn't even realized she'd been away. She was carrying a goshawk whose wing was splinted. Daisy explained, "Mumsy goes deeper into the woods to help those who are more badly sick or injured, who can't make it here on their own. This one will need looking after till the seasons are about to turn."

"That's . . . sweet," Gabriella said. She swallowed the word she'd been about to stick in between those two words: *unexpectedly.* Clearly, it was unexpected only to her. She felt small, and mean-spirited, and useless.

By then the deer mother had picked up her wayward offspring and Mumsy said, sounding deeply weary, "Midday meal in a little bit. I've got to nap."

And Gabriella didn't even think badly of her for that.

"You go ahead and rest, Mumsy," Parf cooed in a slightly-too-solicitous-to-be-believed tone. "You work so hard. Gabby can cook for us."

And Gabriella did think badly of *him* for that.

PHLEG

The rabbit kept Phleg up half the night. Rabbits are nervous, twitchy sleepers, *and* they are most active at dawn and dusk. Just as Phleg was convinced she was exhausted enough to sleep through anything, the rabbit was deciding it was time for grooming and breakfast and more grooming and morning exercises, followed by yet more grooming—and, oh, was there time for a midmorning snack before grooming some more?

"It can't be midmorning if the sun isn't even clear of the horizon yet," Phleg grumbled. Enough was enough. "Go away."

The rabbit did—which left a rapidly cooling spot between her arm and her ribs, where the rabbit had been snuggled against her.

Phleg missed the warmth, but not the constant stirring. Despite the fact that the sun *was* rising, which meant the birds were awake and calling to one another quite noisily—and even though normally her family rose early in order to tend the animals—Phleg was finally able to drift off to a deeper sleep than she had enjoyed all night. She dreamed that she was in the big, comfortable princess bed, and servants were bringing her trayfuls of pastries and sweets and that wonderful sweet milk. In another

97

moment or so, she would sit up and start to eat. The princess's friend Amanda was there, too, directing the servants, calling out, "More food! More food! Princess Phleg needs more food!" It was odd that everyone seemed to know she was Phleg but still called her *princess*, but dreams don't need to make sense to be pleasant.

Or scary, for that matter.

Her brother Parf walked into her dream, and he wasn't bearing food. He kicked one of the legs on which the bed sat, causing the mattress to jiggle. "Wake up!" he commanded.

"Go away," Phleg mumbled at him, or maybe she just thought it—though, in a dream, that should have been enough. But he wasn't as amenable as the rabbit.

He kicked the bed leg again. "Danger!" he said. He kicked again. "Danger!" Kick. "Danger!" Kick. "Danger!"

Now Phleg could hear the vibrations, as well as feel them.

Parf could be an infuriating annoyance, but he was—after all—her brother. Which might or might not mean that something was wrong.

"What?" she demanded, for sure out loud this time. Not just in-her-dream out loud, but in real life—and this woke her up.

Parf was no longer there, but the sounds and vibrations continued.

It was the rabbit, thumping its hind leg in alarm.

Phleg jumped to her feet. As soon as the rabbit saw she was awake, it clearly felt its duty was done and Phleg was on her own now. It dashed off into the underbrush.

Too tall to follow its exact path, Phleg dove in the same direction. She didn't yet know what the danger was but trusted the

98

rabbit, who had seen/heard/smelled or tasted it in the wind. The woodland creature would know which was the best direction in which to flee.

Phleg rolled, putting more distance, more forest vegetation, between her and the clearing where she had settled for the night. Should she get up and run, or hunker low and hide? The answer depended on what the danger was, and Phleg still didn't know.

But then she heard voices. Human voices. Distressingly close by. Calling, "Princess Gabriella!"

Drat! A search party from the castle. Hadn't they given up yet? What was the matter with them?

And then the voices called, "Prince Frederic!"—which was a surprise. Why would they be calling him? Had he run away, too? Given how nasty his father seemed, maybe she shouldn't have been so surprised.

People—two of them, in the uniform of the men who formed the castle guard—entered the clearing with big, noisy, crunch-everything-in-their-path feet.

Phleg peered through the clump of grass where she hid, and winced. Surely, if they were looking for evidence of her passing, they would notice the impression her head had made on that gigantic mushroom she'd been using for a pillow. They would know she had gotten up mere moments before and would realize she must still be in the vicinity. They would find her and return her to the castle, where she absolutely could *not* be, for she was ruining everything for the real princess, and for Prince Fred.

But, no, she was giving the searchers too much credit.

"This is impossible," one of the men told the other. "She could be anywhere in this huge forest. Most like, she's miles away by now."

The other grunted in agreement. "If the beasts haven't eaten her already."

Neither agreeing nor disagreeing with that possibility, the first simply stated, "We'll never find her."

Good, Phleg thought. *Give up. Call off the search.*

"Still"—the second man sighed—"I wouldn't want to be the one to have to tell her parents that."

His companion made a sound of agreement. "Yeah, and I wouldn't want to be the one to have to tell that other king we've gone and lost his son."

Fred? Fred was lost, too?

Well . . . not *too*. She herself was not lost. She simply did not want to be found.

But Fred?

A part of her warmed in pleasure—an even nicer sensation than holding a rabbit: Prince Fred had come looking for her. *Incompetently*, apparently—seeing as he'd gotten himself separated from the others. But still. That wasn't the point. The point was that he'd been concerned about her. Since his father had been set against her, Fred must have defied his father's wishes to join the search for her.

Well, not exactly, she reminded herself.

He had joined in the search for Princess Gabriella. It was just a foolishness gone awry that he thought *she* was Gabriella.

100

The men who were looking for the missing princess and prince paused where they were, so distressingly close to Phleg's hiding spot that she barely dared to breathe. There, they discussed their options. They had been out all night and were tired and hungry. They wanted to return to their own homes, their families, their beds. For all they knew, one of the other parties of searchers might have already found the princess and returned her to the welcome embrace of her parents. True, the church bells were supposed to be rung if that happened, but maybe they had missed the tolling. There was no being certain the sound would carry this far into the woods.

They listened, as though the bells might ring at that very moment.

In the stillness, Phleg heard . . . not bells, but a voice—quiet, or very far away. "Hello," the voice called. "Anyone there?"

Yet another searcher, Phleg surmised. *Give up*, she mentally urged them all. The grass in which she was lying was damp from the morning dew, and she was eager to get up out of it.

The men she was watching apparently could not hear the voice. "And most likely the prince has joined the company of some of the other searchers," one of them speculated. "Which would mean there's no reason for us to continue to tromp through the woods looking for him, either."

The other cupped his hands on either side of his mouth and shouted, "Prince Frederic!"

"Yes!" the distant voice called back. "I'm here!"

Phleg was positioned between where the castle guards stood and where—or rather wherever—Prince Fred was. The two men were scratching their bellies, stamping their feet, chattering to each other, and just generally making enough noise that they couldn't hear the prince. They continued to discuss. They were great discussers. They came to the conclusion that it was probably best not to be the *first* team to return to the castle without either the prince or the princess, and so they would search a little bit longer.

Off they went, away from Phleg, and—also—away from the direction that would have led them to Fred.

Poor Fred, Phleg thought. But surely he wouldn't remain lost for long. As the men she had overheard had said, he'd no doubt connect with other searchers. Eventually.

His voice carried to her once again, fainter, which meant he was moving away from her. "I'm here," he called.

KEEP moving away, Phleg thought. Though she felt sorry for him, because he sounded so discouraged.

"Somebody?" the prince called.

Phleg stood and began drying her dew-damp hands on her skirt.

Was he getting more distant?

Or was his voice fading because he was losing heart?

Without much energy, Fred called, "Anybody?" And then, still listlessly, just on the threshold of her being able to hear, he said, "Help."

What was the matter with people? How had humankind ever survived long enough to build their towns and cities when they were so helpless in the woods?

But she couldn't just leave him, not if he was in trouble. After all, she thought, fairies were supposed to help the sick

102

or injured animals of the forest. A lost prince wasn't that different.

Having her good fairy sense, Phleg could tell which direction she should go even after the prince had stopped calling for help. She also knew just how far she must walk to get there, no matter how the topography of the land forced her to shift her path.

This did not stop her from muttering and complaining to herself all the while she walked toward him.

She found Prince Fred sitting in one of the streams, the water almost up to his chest, and this showed so little sense on his part that she was tempted to leave him there. Though Phleg had been making no attempt to walk quietly, she could tell he was unaware of her, as he was looking down at the water rather than up and around. Phleg could have slipped back between the trees.

But the prince had wrapped his arms around himself, and he was shivering.

Well, she thought, *of course you're shivering. Get up out of the cold water, you ninny.*

What she said was, "If you're looking for me in the stream, I have to tell you: Most princesses wouldn't be hiding underwater."

Fred's head jerked up. "Princess Gabriella! Are you all right?"

It was his combination of joy at seeing her and concern for her well-being that made Phleg look at him more closely. He was sitting at a very odd angle.

"I'm fine," she said. "Are you stuck?"

"Maybe a little bit," he admitted.

She took a step forward.

"Don't come in the water!" the prince warned. "You'll get wet."

Phleg paused, waiting to hear why she *shouldn't* get wet. Perhaps he thought there was something wrong with the water. Her fairy sense told her there was not.

"Well, what do you want me to do?" she asked.

"If you could go back to the castle, and . . . well, first let your parents know you're unharmed—because everyone is so worried. And then—while you're at it—if you could send someone back to fetch me, that would be very much appreciated."

"That would also be a very roundabout way of doing things." Phleg stepped into the water. Cold. That was all that was wrong with it. She sat down.

"Don't . . . ," he started, but then realized she wasn't prepared to listen to him.

There was a half-rotten tree submerged in the stream, evidently carried down from the hills by the winter thaw, and the prince had gotten his foot wedged in it.

"You *are* stuck," she said—rather pointlessly, she realized as soon as the words were out of her mouth. He already knew that. Any of her brothers and most of her sisters would have mocked her for a week.

But Fred's answer was a simple "Yes, I do believe I am."

She tugged and pulled at the trunk, but it wouldn't budge.

"Don't hurt your hands," Fred said. "I've been working at it for most of the night and haven't gotten anywhere."

"Ah!" Phleg said, realizing that Fred's misstep had occurred in the dark. So maybe he wasn't a total ninny. She was glad of that.

"*Ah*, what?" Fred asked.

"Just *ah*."

Fred accepted this. "So, now that you've gotten wet, you see you'll have to go back to our original plan and head off for the castle. I just hope you don't catch a chill."

"It was never our plan," Phleg pointed out. "Just your idea. And, as far as catching a chill, I'm not the one who's been sitting in the stream all night."

"Not *all* night," Fred argued. "Just . . ." He sighed. ". . . most of it. Please get out of the water at least, so the sun can dry you."

Phleg stayed right where she was. In fact, she braced her back against the bank of the stream and put both feet against the trunk of the tree. It wasn't that thick; it was just a beech. But though she was able to break off a branch or two, the trunk stayed where it was. She ducked her head underwater—she could hear Fred telling her not to, even as she did—but seeing exactly what the tree looked like and where its branches were jammed against the earth only convinced her that she would not be able to move it.

"Princess Gabriella!" Fred protested once she came back up.

"Shhh." She looked to the trees that grew nearby and spotted a bullfinch. She whistled for it. Then, when it hopped to a lower branch, she asked of it, "See if you can find any beavers nearby, can you?"

Fred said, "Excuse me?"

105

"I wasn't talking to you." Phleg indicated to the bullfinch, which was already flying away.

Fred nodded as though he thought this made sense. "He understands human speech, does he?"

"*She*," Phleg corrected. "Did you see any red feathers?"

"Um . . ." Fred was taking this as a trick question. "Was I supposed to?"

"Only the males have red. The females are gray."

"So . . ." Fred was trying so hard to understand. ". . . only the females speak human?"

Phleg sighed, since—after all—humans spoke what had originally been fairy speech. "Bullfinches only 'speak' bullfinch. But they can understand a lot. Still, there's a reason many species call erratic, unreliable behavior *flighty*."

"All right, then," Fred said, simply deciding to take her at her word.

"So now we wait," Phleg told him.

"For beavers," Fred agreed.

"Or someone from the castle guard. Or for a woodsman with an ax." She didn't like to think of the castle guard coming, as they would make her return with them. But even more than *that*, she didn't like the way Fred's lips were turning blue, which she suspected meant exactly the same in a human as it would for a fairy.

Phleg put her arm around the prince to help support him and to keep him warm. "Tell me a story," she said, hoping that would keep him occupied. "Like you did for your brother."

Fred considered for a moment, which she thought meant he

106

was trying to settle on which story to tell. But what he said was, "Only if you get out of the water."

"Well, that's not going to happen."

Fred sighed. "You're a lot more bossy and stubborn than I remember."

"Get used to it," Phleg told him.

Chapter 6

Stories

PRINCESS GABRIELLA

The fairy family had no sooner finished eating when a visitor arrived in the kitchen, materializing from a puff of sparkly dust, accompanied by the sound of tiny silver bells. Her clothing—fuchsia and gold and frilly even by royal court standards—was much finer than what Gabriella had seen so far. If the dress and shoes had started as vegetation, their ancestry was skillfully disguised.

Any chance of getting anyone to cooperate in bringing their own dishes to the sink—much less cleaning them—vanished in squeals of "Aunt Sylvimit!" as the children clustered around the newcomer.

"Who is she?" Gabriella whispered to Parf, the only one who held back.

"Aunt Vimit," Parf said. "Think *vomit*."

"I will not," Gabriella told him firmly. "I meant: your mother's sister or your father's?"

"Mumsy's."

This was not the answer Gabriella would have expected, now that she saw the coolness of the fairy women's greeting, which was all quick air kisses and little more than air hugs.

Aunt Sylvimit was slightly more enthusiastic about greeting the children, though she did seem more anxious about her hair and clothing getting mussed than Gabriella felt a favorite aunt should be. Gabriella was just thinking that the children's excitement might be for *any* change in routine, rather than for Sylvimit herself, when the fairy woman glanced in her direction.

"What," she demanded, in a tone that would have been harsh even had she used the more socially acceptable *who*, "is this?"

"Gabby," several of the children shouted, each trying to be the first—or the loudest, or the bounciest—to provide the information.

Gabriella inclined her head and curtseyed in polite greeting, holding out the skirt of her increasingly ragged and decreasingly white nightgown. "Princess Gabriella of—"

Before Gabriella could finish, Mumsy cut in, "She's our changeling." She seemed eager to provide even more details, starting, "There's a long tradition—"

"Changeling?" Sylvimit took her own turn at interrupting. "Isn't she rather *old*?" She said *old* as though the word hurt her mouth, in the same tone someone might say *dirty*. "And . . ." Gabriella braced herself to once again be called *big*. ". . . *bulky*?"

Bulky? That was even worse than *big*. For someone who—until meeting the fairies—had most often been described as *petite*, the word stung. Gabriella resolved to think of the fairy woman as

Vimit rather than *Sylvimit* from now on. She couldn't bring herself to manage *Vomit*.

"Most irregular," Vimit muttered disapprovingly. She cast a sour look over her nieces and nephews, clearly counting. She must not have been able to place who was missing. "Who's she been changed for?"

"Phleg," the chorus of eager young fairy voices informed her.

Vimit's brows creased in concentration or criticism. "Renphlegena," she corrected, snapping her wings in disapproval. "Your sister has a beautiful and distinguished name she shares with her beautiful and distinguished great-grandmother. It should not be shortened to something so . . ." She sniffed—she actually *sniffed*. ". . . so . . . unattractive . . . and . . . unrefined." These words, too, seemed to hurt her mouth. "I don't know what's the matter with this family of yours, Luna," she told Mumsy. "First that worthless husband of yours, now this."

Gabriella had heard Mumsy call her husband "no account" and "useless" on several occasions, but apparently she reserved that right for herself.

"First," Mumsy said, "the institution of *changelings* is a time-honored practice. And second, if Benlos and I are interested in humans and their customs, that's really no concern of yours." Several of the children nodded emphatically, though Gabriella doubted Mumsy had ever shown the slightest interest in humans until that very moment.

Vimit gave an I-know-something-you-don't smile. "You might not feel that way once the Fairy Council has its say."

Mumsy was struggling to rise above this goading, Gabriella

110

could tell by her tight lips, but in the end she could not. "Go on and tell me, then," she snapped.

"Benlos has gone and gotten himself in trouble." Vimit sounded quite pleased to be the bearer of bad news.

Little Miss-mot seemed to take in the unease of her older siblings. She either threw herself to the ground or fell, and she began to howl. Gabriella picked her up, since with Mumsy distracted no one else seemed inclined to, and tried to jiggle her into a better mood.

"Trouble," Mumsy said to Vimit, "which *your* husband, being on the Council, could probably get him out of."

"Oh no," Vimit hastened to say. "No, no, no. Not without the risk of tarnishing his own reputation."

Parf snorted. "And Uncle Ardforgel would never do that for *this* side of the family."

"Priorities," Vimit said, by which Gabriella took her to mean, *You're right about that.* "Nonetheless, I just thought you would want to know." Vimit's smile was more sincere this time. Sincere—and, Gabriella felt, perhaps a bit unduly cheerful, given the situation. "Toodles." She fluttered her wings so that she hovered, hummingbird style, a foot or two above the ground. Once again, Gabriella could hear diminutive bells.

"Wait!" Mumsy said. "What sort of trouble?"

"What do you think? Besides, I already said: Trouble because of his interest in humans. Not only that, but—as you should be able to guess—with thieving. Thinking he can get by on good looks and charm alone, even though that mostly seems to work on you." She disappeared in a flash of pinkish-purple

111

shimmer. Gabriella took this to be a mode of fairy transportation, rather than assuming Vimit had exploded. Unpleasant as Mumsy's sister was, surely exploding in front of the family would have brought some reaction beyond Mumsy's, "Oooh, that woman!"

Several of the children echoed her, eager to show their support.

Mumsy turned to Gabriella. "You're going to have to stay here and watch the children," she said, "while Parhenoloff and I go sort this out."

It took Gabriella a moment to decipher that *Parhenoloff* was Parf's full name, his real name. She was just nodding and beginning to say, "It would be my honor—"

—When Parf told Mumsy, "You should stay with the little ones, and I should go with Gabby."

"What?" Mumsy asked. "Why?"

Gabriella would have asked the same questions, except she was momentarily stunned into silence.

Parf rubbed his nose and scuffed his feet on the kitchen floor, and finally said, "She's smart."

"And I'm not?" Mumsy demanded.

Most of the children sensibly chose this moment to tiptoe into other parts of the house.

Without looking at either Mumsy or Gabriella, Parf said, "She's smart in the way of the Council."

"I doubt it," Mumsy snapped. "She's never even stood before the Council."

"Any more than you have," Parf agreed. "But she has a way with words. Of . . . I don't know . . . of making nice. Like Uncle

112

Ardforgel." Now he did look up at Gabriella. "I don't mean that as a compliment."

"Then I shall not take it as one," Gabriella said. But it was still a surprise to have him acknowledge her as having a skill.

"You know you'll get all upset and start yelling," Parf told Mumsy, "and that won't help. Gabby wouldn't yell if her hair was on fire. She's a princess. She knows about these things. Not about hair being on fire," he hastened to add, misinterpreting the quizzical look Gabriella was giving him, "but about talking people into and out of things. She knows these things. Even if"—he again hastened to add, because Mumsy looked ready to interrupt—"she doesn't know about these things from a fairy standpoint."

Mumsy was considering. "You're certainly making your point about *you* being inarticulate," she told Parf. She looked at Gabriella. "You're a princess . . . ?"

Gabriella nodded.

". . . And as such are used to speaking in public?"

"I've had lessons from earliest childhood in elocution, law, and logic." *But, still,* Gabriella thought, even as she tried to squelch the little voice of doubt and worry, *not fairy law and logic.*

How different could it be?

There was a crash from another part of the house, and one or more of the children started howling.

Mumsy looked at Parf levelly. "This is your father's life we're talking about."

"Understood."

Clearly, Mumsy was still undecided, weighing things in her head. "You don't much like your father."

Parf shrugged. "Neither do you." Before she could protest, he continued, "But he is my father. And if he's in some sort of trouble because of humans, who better than a human—?"

"Muuummmmsyyyy," several of the children bawled, though they sounded more annoyed with one another than in need of medical assistance.

Mumsy waved a dismissal. "Go," she told Parf and Gabriella. "This is such a nuisance. Simply getting you there will take just about all the magic I've managed to save up."

"You save up magic?" Gabriella asked. There was so much she didn't know about fairies.

But at the same moment, she realized there had been more to Mumsy's gesture than just a wave of dismissal. Gabriella and Parf were—as Aunt Vimit had been only moments earlier—floating free of the ground.

And then Gabriella felt herself dissolve—which was *not* a pleasant sensation, despite the sparkles.

PHLEG

"Tell me a story," Phleg said to Prince Fred as they waited for the beavers to come to the rescue.

Fred looked confused. Phleg had already noticed that he often looked confused. But she didn't hold this against him. "What kind of story?" he asked.

"Doesn't matter. It's just to pass the time." She didn't add, *And to keep you from worrying.*

Of course, *she* was worrying, too. She wished she had asked the bullfinch to fly back with a report. It would be nice to know when the looking-for-beavers stage was over and the help-was-on-its-way part of the waiting had started. Then all she'd need to be concerned about was if help was likely to come sooner (should the beavers live in this particular stream) or later (if they lived on another body of water and had to travel overland, rather than being able to swim all the way).

"I don't really know any stories," Fred said.

"Of course you do," Phleg insisted. "I heard you tell your brother a story."

Fred blushed. "Oh. That was just something I made up." He looked as though this was a bad thing. "I'm terrible at telling *real* stories. I keep forgetting bits—important bits—and then I have to go back and say, 'Oh, did I mention the monster only had one eye?' When I'm making up stories, it's easier."

Phleg shook her head. "Seems to me it would be harder."

Fred thought for a moment, trying to work out if she could be right. Then he said, "No, easier. I have to admit, Gabriella: I'm not the smartest prince in the royal family."

"That's a sad thing to say, considering Telmund is less than half your age."

Fred laughed as though she were joking. "Well, but there's my three older brothers, too. Don't forget them."

Phleg hadn't seen any older brothers. She'd assumed there was only Fred and Telmund. Not that she could admit that, since Gabriella probably knew. She was about to say that *of course* she hadn't forgotten them, but Fred's solemn face convinced her not

115

to try bluffing about what she knew and didn't know. "I forget things, too," she admitted.

"Everybody does," Fred assured her.

Phleg poked his arm with her finger. "See? So you can't go around saying that forgetting makes you not-the-smartest-prince-in-the-royal-family."

Fred shook his head and opened his mouth to argue, then let the subject drop.

"So," Phleg said, "that story you told your brother: It was good. It had action, and adventure, and I really liked the main character. And I liked that things worked out, even when another adventure was starting. When my brother tells stories, he intentionally tries to upset us: to scare us, or to make us cry."

Fred blinked. Twice. He said, "But you're an only child."

Nitwit! Phleg chided herself. *You're as slow as pudding!* "Well," she said, "but sometimes I imagine I have a brother and he torments me."

"That is inventive of you." Fred sounded caught between admiration and not-sure-whether-he-was-being-made-fun-of. "Most people make up an imaginary friend to keep them company."

"Well, Parf does do that. It's just bad company."

Fred laughed again. "Sometimes my brothers are bad company, too. They tell me making up stories is for dreamers who can't do anything else."

"Well, they're just wrong." It was hard to believe, but there were a few fairies who thought like that, too. "My father tells stories," she added. "They're a lot better than my brother's. Some he's made up himself, others are ones he's heard. I

116

like the stories, but he travels to gather them, so he isn't home much."

Fred was wearing his confused look again. "That must be difficult, for a king," he observed.

Phleg stood up and shielded her eyes as though she was looking for the beavers. *Mush for brains!* she chided herself. *You're supposed to be Princess Gabriella.* She admitted to Fred, "Still, I understand what it's like to forget the important bits."

It took him a moment to catch up, but then he nodded. "Once upon a time," he started.

"Drat!" Phleg said.

Fred looked crestfallen. "You don't like stories that begin 'Once upon a time . . .'?" he asked.

"What?" Phleg said. "No. I mean, *yes.* I mean, *no,* that isn't what I meant because, *yes,* I like stories that begin 'Once upon a time . . .' But the beavers are here."

"We were waiting for the beavers," Fred pointed out.

"So we were." To the pair of beavers who were swimming downstream, Phleg said, "Thank you for coming. I know this is a busy season for you. I hope you didn't have far to travel, but my friend has gotten caught by this tree. I figured you'd be much faster about getting him loose than people ever could be."

It took several seconds for Fred to be able to close his mouth. Apparently he hadn't really believed that beavers were coming to help him. Which was both annoying (since it indicated he thought Phleg hadn't known what she was talking about) and flattering (since he had been sitting here calmly talking with her anyway).

The beavers—a young male and female, probably in their first summer together—dove underwater and assessed the situation. In no time, they had settled on the best place to start chewing.

In no time plus just a little, they worked their way through the trunk.

"Oh," Fred said, feeling the obstruction give. He leaned backward and wiggled his foot out from under the trunk, and then swung his leg free of the branches that still wanted to snag him.

"Here," Phleg said, "don't put weight on that until we know it isn't broken." She stood and took hold of him under his arms, dragging him back even as he was trying to get his feet under him.

"You're strong for such a delicate thing," Fred told her.

Which was odd, considering what a lumbering big girl Princess Gabriella was.

Well, Phleg realized, maybe not if you compared her to other people, rather than to fairies.

She said, "Sometimes people take you by surprise."

With Phleg tugging and Fred scooting backward, they soon had him up on the bank, entirely out of the water.

"Thank you," Phleg called after the beavers, who were already swimming back upstream.

Fred added his voice to hers. "I really appreciate it—especially this being your busy season and all!"

The beavers smacked their tails against the water to let him know he was welcome.

"Why *is* this the busy season for beavers?" Fred asked Phleg.

"All seasons are the busy season for beavers," she told him. She called one more thing after them: "If you come across a wolf or a deer, or a sheep that has wandered away from its human keepers, or some other big mammal that can help keep us warm, would you send it over?" She thought another moment, then added, "Goats are acceptable, but no porcupines!" Then she turned back to Fred. "Let me see your leg."

Clearly the last thing she'd said to the beavers had startled him, so he was entirely taken by surprise when she set her hand on his knee.

"Oh, I'm not sure—" Fred started.

"Hush," Phleg told him, firmly enough that he did.

There was no blood, so she knew he hadn't been gashed, but she needed to see if anything was broken. She gently ran her fingers down his shin, and she made him twirl his foot to confirm that it still worked.

"See, I'm fine," he told her.

"You are not. There's a crack running lengthwise on your shinbone."

Fred touched the area she indicated. "I don't feel it."

"You're not an expert. And you *will* feel it if you try to walk. So we need to wait here for people-help after all." That did not please her, but there was nothing she could do about it. She wasn't going to desert him.

She knew that once Fred calmed down, he would start to feel the cold from having spent the night in the stream. His leg would start to ache from the battering it had received. Too bad she didn't have her mother's talent for making clothes out of

119

what nature provided, so that she could give him something dry to wear. Phleg also wished for the store of powdered herbs and prepared unguents that would be at home. Instead she had to make do with some betony growing on the bank of the stream.

"Chew the leaves," she told Fred. "It will help with the pain."

"I'm not in pain," Fred objected. But it seemed all he had needed was the thought put in his head. He began to chew the leaves.

He didn't even notice—Phleg suspected there was a lot Fred didn't notice—when the bear appeared, shambling through the woods.

What happened next was Phleg's own fault. "Oh," Phleg said, "here's a bear."

Fred gulped, swallowing the betony leaf, and began choking.

Phleg thumped Fred on the back at the same time she motioned for the bear that it was safe to approach.

Of course animals are not fooled by spells, so it saw *her*, not Princess Gabriella. Still, normally it would have been nervous to draw near Fred, but once it realized that he presented no danger and, in fact, was in trouble, the bear did come. It even joined Phleg in pounding the prince on the back. This only helped until Fred realized there was too much back-pounding going on to all be from one person. Still coughing, he tried to scramble backward at the same time he threw his arms up to protect Phleg.

Phleg realized that the bear *might be* a bit intimidating to someone who didn't know him. "Don't worry," Phleg said. "This bear and I are old friends."

"You're what?" Fred asked, the paleness of his skin and the hugeness of his eyes indicating he wasn't convinced.

"I helped him when he was a cub," Phleg told Fred, at the same time she patted the bear on the snout. "He broke his leg in a fall—an injury very similar to yours—so it's especially nice that he's come here to help you."

"You what?" Fred asked. "He what? What what?"

"Oh, hush," Phleg told him, since that had worked before. "I can't keep you warm all by myself."

"I'm not cold," Fred said.

She *could* have believed that his teeth were chattering more from fear than cold, but the prince's lips were blue.

"Well, I am," Phleg said. "Cold and wet. Besides, didn't your mother ever give you bear hugs?"

"No," Fred said. "I had a nanny."

The bear didn't take offense and sat down next to him anyway. He enveloped both Fred and Phleg in a nice, warm, only slightly smelly bear hug.

"I'm a bit squished," Fred said, gasping for breath and eyeing the long, sharp claws at the ends of the bear's paws.

"Oh, stop feeling sorry for yourself," Phleg told him. "You were about to tell me a story. You might want to make sure there's a part in it about a nice, helpful bear ..."

121

Chapter 7

Councils and Rescue Parties

PRINCESS GABRIELLA

Materializing after Mumsy's transportation spell was as uncomfortable as dissolving had been. Gabriella, who as part of her Servants and Their Work unit of study had helped prepare a meal in the castle's kitchen, remembered the feeling of scraping her knuckles against a cheese grater. This felt like that. Except all over.

Once the sparkly, gritty fog disappeared, the scene in front of her wobbled before settling, and at the same time there was a sound like a gong. Gabriella assumed that was because Mumsy's spells weren't as sophisticated as Aunt Vimit's, so a gong was Mumsy's version of the delicate tinkling of bells. But Parf said, "Just in time. That was the summons for the Council."

The fact that he could speak showed that Parf had known to hold his breath. Since he had neglected to warn Gabriella to do so, she was too busy coughing on the coarse sparkles to answer.

They were in a room as huge as any of the public gathering places in the castle, but circular, as at Mumsy's. Apparently all fairies favored walls made from glittery, pastel-colored stones, but here the pale colors—pinks, lavenders, mauves, blues, and greens—shifted and blended, constantly moving, like wisps of cloud or eddies of colors in a dye vat. While the basic look of the room was similar to Mumsy's, only grander, the clothing worn by the dozen or so fairies in this room was nothing like what Gabriella had seen so far—it was gauzy and swirly, and none of it looked vegetative. Both men and women favored crowns of flowers entwined around golden circlets. All in all, they showed that Vimit's style was not out of the ordinary—Mumsy's was.

Only a few of the fairies glanced in the direction of the spot where Gabriella and Parf had suddenly appeared, evidence that such comings and goings were not especially noteworthy. Those who *did* look seemed more taken aback about the fact that Parf had a human with him, rather than that he had appeared out of a damp dust cloud. Gabriella hoped they didn't know enough about humans to recognize that she was dressed in a nightgown. But most seemed as unconcerned about the two of them as about the Council-summoning bell, and even those who *had* spared a moment to glance continued chatting in small groups, or strolling in whichever direction they had been going all along.

"Wait!" Gabriella caught hold of Parf's arm as he took a step toward one of the entryways. It was an impulsive and presumptuous action, and she immediately let go. But not before noticing that, though he was wiry, his arm was solid and strong. Not that this had anything to do with anything.

Though it was the last reaction she would have ever expected, he blushed as his eyes flicked to where her hand had rested.

Was he embarrassed that she'd touched him—or annoyed at the impertinence?

She covered her own uncomfortable feelings by asking, "What can you explain to prepare me?"

Whatever Parf was feeling didn't come through in his voice. "You were there when Vomit came," he said. "You know as much as I do."

"I do not," Gabriella protested. "You know the whole background, the history of what's going on. You know *why* you suggested I should come."

"I already said: You talk good." Parf sighed. "You're like my father, and like Uncle Ardforgel: You use words to twist what is and to make everyone see what isn't. And to get everyone to do what you want."

"I don't . . . That's not . . . How can you . . . ?"

Parf raised an eyebrow, perhaps thinking, *Well, maybe you don't talk THAT good.* "Like getting the little-uns to like you, which is no big deal, but getting them to do your kitchen cleanup for you. Like getting Mumsy to like you."

Gabriella took a deep breath. There were so many things she could have said, objections she could have made. Mumsy liked her? She had to choose. "You make it sound like words are used to deceive and control. People *can* use words like that; I imagine fairies can, too. But mostly words help us to communicate."

Parf shrugged. "You always say exactly what you mean? What you're thinking?"

This would have been easier to answer before she had met him and his family.

In any case, he didn't give her time. "Never mind," he told her. "Come communicate in front of the Council."

None of the doorways before them were marked, and they all seemed to lead outdoors, to some tranquil green, leafy place. Gabriella wondered how well Parf knew his way around here—wherever *here* was. He took hold of her arm just as they passed the closest threshold—and she couldn't help wondering: Did he do this to disconcert her in retaliation for how she'd disconcerted him? Not that she would allow herself to become flustered . . .

"Council," he said, and this time it was the scene in front of them, not they themselves, that dissolved. When the surroundings returned a heartbeat later, Gabriella and Parf were standing in a different room. And surely, she told herself, it was the there-then-not-there-then-there-again nature of their location that accounted for the tingly sensation in her arm, not the fact that Parf was holding it. Still, that reasoning did nothing to keep *her* from blushing.

As with all the fairy rooms she had seen so far, this was yet again circular. But this one had only one door, the one through which they'd just come. Except, when Gabriella looked back, the view was no longer the large gathering room but the same glimpse of woodsiness through which they must have passed, but had not.

Parf tugged on her arm to get her to look forward. Though by no means cramped, the room was much smaller than the vast one where they had just been. It was occupied by a single round table, at which five fairies sat, two women and three men.

Someone had probably been talking, Gabriella guessed by the way the air seemed suddenly still. Those four facing the doorway looked at her and Parf with a range of expressions, from mystification to fierceness. The fifth fairy, who had his back to them, glanced in their direction, then turned fully around to smile broadly at them.

"Parhenoloff!" He jumped to his feet. "This is my son!" he explained to the others in a delighted-sounding voice. "And . . ." looking at Gabriella, but still sounding delighted, ". . . I have no idea!"

"Gabby," Parf mumbled. "Her name's Gabby. She's our changeling."

"We haven't had a changeling in ages!" Parf's father said in a tone indicating it was high time they fix that.

Gabriella remembered Sylvimit accusing the children's father of getting by on good looks and charm, and she immediately could see how that could be. He was supposed to be in trouble, but no one would ever guess that from the twinkle in his eye and his welcoming manner. He acted as though he had never been happier to meet anyone. "Pull up the chair," he said in invitation, which got a sour look from most of the Council members.

"Benlos," one of the male Council members said disapprovingly, "this is most irregular."

There was a single extra chair, tucked out of the way by the wall, but when Parf pulled it out and placed it next to where his father was sitting, another chair appeared where the first had been. Gabriella blinked. She had the impression that the table had shimmered, but didn't catch what exactly had happened. It

126

was only when Parf pulled that second chair to the table that she could ignore the sudden appearance of yet another chair by the wall, and actually see that the whole table had meanwhile expanded, growing larger to accommodate the new seats.

One of the female Council members, the one wearing the biggest scowl, spoke up. "We will allow this, Benlos, so long as your . . ." She sucked her teeth. ". . . family . . ." That word was spoken with an even more impressive scowl. ". . . is not a disruption."

"Absolutely," Benlos agreed, with a winning smile. Only it did not win over the Council.

"No human shenanigans," warned the male fairy who hadn't spoken yet. It was not the well-mannered greeting Gabriella might have expected from someone evidently highly placed in the fairy world. "We don't want these proceedings to drag on longer than necessary, as we have other important business."

Judging by his sleepy eyes and his stifled yawn, Gabriella had a good idea what "important business" might be in his immediate future. She mentally dubbed him Close to Napping Fairy Man.

Still: "No shenanigans," she agreed, politely but not meekly. She smiled at each of the Council members. They were not won over by *her* smile, either.

She sat next to Parf, who sat next to his father. On her left side was the first male fairy, who seemed to be vying with the woman fairy who'd already spoken for the sourest expression in the room. Parf was a close third.

The woman fairy, who seemed to be in charge, said, "To resume, after this inopportune interruption: Benlos, you have been caught stealing some of Councillor Ardforgel's dragons'

127

teeth, purportedly to fund your expeditions into the human world in order to collect . . ." Again she sucked her teeth. ". . . stories."

Gabriella had resolved that her best strategy was to sit quietly until she fully understood the situation. That plan didn't last long. "Excuse me—his what?"

There was a loud sigh from the fairy that Gabriella was quickly beginning to think of as Irate Fairy Woman (as distinguished from only Moderately Annoyed Fairy Woman, who hadn't spoken yet, and Irate Fairy Man and Close to Napping Fairy Man). Irate Fairy Woman repeated, enunciating slowly and carefully, "Dragons' teeth."

"Ardforgel has a dragon?" Gabriella asked. "And Benlos stole its teeth?" That seemed brave, though foolhardy. And unfortunate for the dragon. Also, she couldn't begin to imagine why Benlos would have done such a thing.

Irate Fairy Man snorted so energetically he had to turn his face and discreetly dab at his nose.

Parf groaned in exasperation. "Fairies don't keep animals," he reminded Gabriella in a mutter under his breath.

"Doesn't this changeling know anything about fairies?" Irate Fairy Woman demanded. Her wings flicked and snapped in irritation.

"She's new," Parf explained.

"I think she's doing fabulously." Benlos craned around his son to give Gabriella a nod of encouragement.

Moderately Annoyed Fairy Woman said to Gabriella, "Not Ardforgel's personal dragon. His personal supply of teeth, gathered from dragons."

"Wow," Gabriella said, feeling a grudging respect for Ardforgel.

Moderately Annoyed Fairy Woman clearly saw what Gabriella was thinking and felt it was her duty to set the record straight for the human visitor. "Fairies gather the baby teeth that dragons shed as they grow." Seeing Gabriella take a breath to ask, she added, "Those teeth are the source of most fairy magic."

"I didn't know that," Gabriella said.

All four members of the Council said, "Obviously."

"Still," Gabriella said, "baby teeth? Wouldn't teeth from full-grown dragons be more powerful?"

Irate Fairy Woman slammed her hand on the table as though her patience had been exhausted.

"And," Gabriella guessed, "that would make them harder to come by. Sorry. I won't interrupt again."

The fairies seemed to relax.

"Except," Gabriella said, "sorry, one more question." Despite all the sighs from the Council members, she asked, "So what do you do with the teeth? Grind them up into . . . fairy dust?" She was thinking of the way Vimit had come and gone in a cloud of shimmery dust.

"Dust?" Irate Fairy Man repeated, since Irate Fairy Woman was clearly so beside herself with vexation that she was beyond words. *"Dust?* Do humans use dust to trade?"

"No," Gabriella admitted hesitantly. "But we don't use teeth, either."

Parf put his face down on the table, grumbling, "I'm so glad I brought you."

His father said, "Hush now," and he leaned across to pat Gabriella's hand, plainly offering comfort. "You're doing the best you can," he said. "That's the important thing."

"Really?" Parf asked his father. "I would have thought the important thing was not having you exiled." He sat up, his wings quivering. "Or is that what you want? To have an excuse to leave us and go live among the humans?"

"No," Benlos said, sounding genuinely shocked at the idea. "Leave the family?"

Irate Fairy Woman had finally gotten her voice back. "Did I not say *No disruptions*? Another interruption from you, Changeling, and I will fine your family and have you cast out."

Judging by Parf's stricken look, when she said *family* she meant *fairy family*, and—again judging by his look—they didn't have the . . . well, the teeth . . . to pay a fine.

She nodded, even though she felt that, strictly speaking, it would be politer to say out loud that she understood; but she worried that, given the fairies' mood, they might count even agreement as an interruption.

Irate Fairy Woman drummed her thin fingers on the table— perhaps waiting for verbal acknowledgment. Perhaps waiting to pounce on Gabriella.

Gabriella gave what she hoped was a winsome smile.

Irate Fairy Woman sighed, then turned to Irate Fairy Man and said, "Councillor Ardforgel, please explain to the Council what happened."

Irate Fairy Man was Ardforgel? And he was a member of the Council? Gabriella had attended sessions when her father sat in

130

judgment and weighed testimony from two conflicting parties. She bit her lip to keep from blurting out: *This is a clear case of conflict of interest.*

Ardforgel said, "Benlos had come to my home to visit. As he is . . ." Arforgel sniffed, and Gabriella wondered if he had picked up that mannerism from his wife, or she from him. ". . . as he is my wife's sister's husband . . ." He rolled his eyes to show what he thought of *that.* ". . . I felt family-bound to ask him in."

"So you had not invited him?" Moderately Annoyed Fairy Woman asked. "He simply stopped by, unannounced?"

"That is correct," Ardforgel said.

Benlos made a noise somewhere between a *hmmm* and a snort, then smiled apologetically as though the sound had been unintentional.

"Now is not the time for your testimony," Irate Fairy Woman admonished.

Benlos nodded somberly, but then winked at her.

She was not amused.

"*Anyway*," Ardforgel said, fighting to regain everyone's attention, "since I know Benlos and his family have hardly enough dragons' teeth to fill the mouth of a chicken, and since this means he has to . . ." Ardforgel shuddered. ". . . *walk* everywhere, I invited him to sit and rest and have a refreshing lemonade. While I went into the kitchen, Benlos sat in our parlor." He nodded meaningfully.

Irate Fairy Woman asked, "And that's where you keep your dragons' teeth?"

131

"Well, not *all*." Ardforgel's tone indicated such a possibility would be ridiculous. "*Some* of them. About a dozen. A handy supply for impulsive or whimsical spells." As he said this, he rested his hand against his upper chest, just below his neck.

Though Gabriella hadn't asked—she hadn't dared—Benlos leaned around Parf to explain. He pulled a locket, somewhat battered and the worse for wear, from beneath his own shirt. "We all have one of these—"

The Council members were nodding, and Gabriella could make out the shape of a locket or two beneath each fairy's clothing. But Ardforgel snorted.

"Yes, yes," Benlos said, "we all know your locket is much finer than mine." Once he flipped it open, Gabriella saw a single sharp tooth, about as big as her pinkie. "The magic wears out," he said. "Some fairies go through significantly more teeth than others of us do."

Gabriella nodded before glancing at the Council members and drawing her finger across her lips. She crossed her arms to say, without ever actually saying, *Not a word passed my lips. You can't accuse me of disrupting.*

"Some of us," Ardforgel snapped, "work hard for our dragons' teeth."

"Certainly," Benlos said. "And some of us had *parents* who worked hard, then passed *their* dragons' teeth on to us—and yet are *still* greedy and ever-conniving for more."

Apparently this was a sensitive subject for Ardforgel. "And some of us are lazy wastrels who squander what we have, and couldn't hold on to dragons' teeth even . . . even if your hands were covered in sap!"

Close to Napping Fairy Man looked as though Ardforgel's raised voice might have jerked him back from the very precipice of, in fact, napping. "Must you be so loud in your convictions?" he asked.

Moderately Annoyed Fairy Woman tapped her fingers against the table. "In any case, this is not the time nor place for this discussion."

"But you can see," Arforgel persisted, "that Benlos resents my good fortune and feels entitled to it himself."

Gabriella permitted a little squeak to escape from the back of her throat as the two fairy women looked at each other. Irate Fairy Woman was nodding at what Ardforgel had just said, but Moderately Annoyed Fairy Woman, after a quick glance at Gabriella, admitted, "Not exactly."

"Well, he does," Ardforgel muttered.

Irate Fairy Woman told him, "Continue telling what happened."

Ardforgel was pouting, but he finished, "I came back from the kitchen, and the cabinet where we store some just-for-whims teeth was open. Benlos was gone. And so were the teeth."

Irate Fairy Woman turned to Parf's father. "And what do you have to say for yourself?"

"There's not much of that account with which I would agree," Benlos said. "Starting with: Ardforgel and I crossed paths in the Everywhere Room—and he invited me to accompany him to his house."

The Everywhere Room, Gabriella surmised, must be the room where she and Parf had ended up after Mumsy's spell. The room itself was clearly magical, so that fairies could use it to get from one place to wherever they wanted to be. Very handy magic.

Benlos continued. "He said his wife was gone for the day—either shopping for yet more clothing and useless objects to make herself feel important, or flitting from friend to friend, gathering and dispersing gossip. He said we would have plenty of time to talk without her interruptions."

"Lies," Ardforgel sputtered.

Irate Fairy Woman told him, "You will have another chance to speak anon."

Gabriella gave an emphatic nod to show her kindly-note-that-I'm-still-not-talking support for this fair ruling.

Ardforgel squirmed in his chair, clearly wanting a chance to speak both now *and* anon.

Benlos continued. "Ardforgel told me his wife goes through dragons' teeth faster than hummingbirds go through nectar."

"I would never!" Ardforgel protested.

Close to Napping Fairy Man said, "Councillor Ardforgel, you're bruising my eardrums. You're more bothersome than the changeling."

Gabriella smiled as endearingly as she could manage.

"Is there any purpose to what you're saying," Irate Fairy Woman asked Benlos, "other than to belittle Sylvimit?"

Benlos paused to weigh the question—perhaps he thought belittling Sylvimit might be reason enough. But then he said, "Ardforgel is running short of dragons' teeth. Well, running short by *his* standards. He heard me tell a story—and by *story*, I mean I never tried to pass it off as something real—about a magic cauldron. Though I do admit my stories are very compelling." Benlos paused and considered. "Gripping, even. And logical—and by that I mean internally consistent. And therefore believable. And—"

Ardforgel jumped to his feet. "You are so full of yourself!" he cried.

Benlos shrugged. "In the story," he said, "whatever anyone put into that cauldron at night, come morning you would find two of the thing. He offered to buy this cauldron from me."

"This makes no sense," Moderately Annoyed Fairy Woman said. "If you had such a cauldron, why wouldn't *you* use it? Why would you be poor?"

Good for you! Gabriella thought, hoping the fairy woman might be more on Benlos's side than the others.

Benlos inclined his head. "As you say," he murmured, "no one has ever accused Ardforgel of being particularly gifted in the realm of common sense. But he did ask for proof. He gave me this one tooth . . ." His hand brushed against the locket. ". . . and he told me to bring two back. I admit only that I felt no guilt in taking his tooth. Anyone that foolish . . ." Benlos shrugged and gave a sheepish grin. "One could almost make a case for such a person deserving to be taken advantage of . . . in a small matter . . . to teach him to be more discerning."

Probably not the best defense, Gabriella thought.

In fact, Irate Fairy Woman brought her hand down on the table, making everyone—not just Close to Napping Fairy Man—jump. "Enough of this sniping at each other," she ordered.

135

"Ardforgel, sit down. Was there anyone present by your home to see you invite Benlos in?"

"No," Ardforgel admitted.

Turning to Benlos, she asked, "Was anyone present in the Everywhere Room when Ardforgel invited you to his home?"

Benlos shook his head. "No one who would have noticed us."

"Then it seems to me," Irate Fairy Woman said, "that it's a case of you-say-this-and-*you*-say-that. Each of you claims one version of events, and neither of you can prove anything. It is one fairy's word against another."

"Except," Moderately Annoyed Fairy Woman reminded them, "for the fact that Benlos has a dragon's tooth he admits is Ardforgel's."

So much for being on Benlos's side.

The fairies all nodded grimly.

"One," Benlos pointed out.

"I don't know what he did with the other eleven," Ardforgel hurried to say. "Beyond the fact that he obviously spent one on a changeling spell."

From the beginning of her stay, Gabriella had had the impression that the fairy children were responsible for her being there. She jabbed Parf in the ribs.

He yipped in surprise, then glowered at her for calling attention to him.

"Everyone's looking at you now anyway," Gabriella muttered at him.

Nervous to speak before the Council members, he still managed to mutter loud enough to be heard, "It was Phleg done that. She used her own dragon's tooth." He faced Ardforgel. "The one you and Aunt Vo"—he corrected himself—"Aunt Vimit gave for her coming-of-age ceremony. The chipped one."

A chipped dragon's tooth had to be less valuable than a whole one, and Gabriella noticed eyebrows went up around the room at Ardforgel's patent tightfistedness. "Be that as it may . . . ," Ardforgel blustered.

"It seems to me," Irate Fairy Woman forged on, "that given the total lack of evidence or witnesses, we can only judge by the character of those involved." She paused to let everyone think about that.

Gabriella's heart sank.

"So," Irate Fairy Woman said, "we need to decide: Do we trust the word of a respected member of the Council, who comes from a long line of distinguished ancestors? Or of a . . . Storyteller . . . And bear in mind that *Storyteller* means someone who makes up stories. Or, put another way, someone who tells lies."

Gabriella glanced around the room. The Council members were all nodding or shaking their heads at precisely the wrong moments—except for Close to Napping Fairy Man, who was nodding at everything, clearly about to drop off.

Parf would not look up from his hands, clasped on the table. Even Benlos appeared deflated.

"A vote," Irate Fairy Woman declared, clearly hoping to be loud enough to bestir those Council members whose chins were drooping toward their chests. "Who believes Ardforgel?" Her own hand went up as she asked.

Ardforgel's hand shot up.

More slowly, Moderately Annoyed Fairy Woman raised her hand.

Irate Fairy Woman nudged Close to Napping Fairy Man, who—seeing all the other hands raised—raised his own.

Irate Fairy Woman made a show of counting each of the Council members.

"And who," she asked, letting her hand drop, "believes Benlos?"

Gabriella raised her hand.

"You are not allowed to vote!" snapped both Irate Fairy Woman and Ardforgel.

Gabriella jumped to her feet. "This is unfair," she told them. Parf was making all sorts of grimaces and twitches for her to sit back down. "I know it's rude to be dismissive of other cultures, but fairy law is unfair."

"No, it's not," Irate Fairy Woman said dismissively.

But Moderately Annoyed Fairy Woman asked, "How so?"

"Ardforgel is the one making the complaint. How can he be allowed to vote?"

"Even so," Ardforgel drawled, "it's still three who believe me, and that leaves . . . let's see . . . how many believe Benlos? Oh yes, that would be *none*."

Gabriella said, "That's because nobody has been asking the right questions."

His voice dripping with scorn, Ardforgel asked, "The right questions being those relating to personal dragons and fairy dust?"

"No," Gabriella said, drawing the word out as she realized she had worked herself into a corner.

"What should we be asking?" asked Moderately Annoyed

Fairy Woman, the only Council member who seemed even remotely interested in the truth.

Gabriella took a deep breath. She realized that if she was to save Benlos, then she must let her courtly training overcome her fear of doing something wrong. She had seen her father settle disputes. She could do this. "Clearly, the most important question is: Who has something to gain from all of this?"

Ardforgel made a sound of exasperation. "*Clearly . . . ,*" he said, mimicking Gabriella. He looked around the room to ensure that everyone was with him—and everyone was, right down to Close to Napping Fairy Man, who didn't even complain about Ardforgel's escalating volume. ". . . clearly, the answer is THE PERSON WHO HAS MORE DRAGONS' TEETH NOW THAN BEFORE."

"But," Gabriella persisted, "who would that be?"

Ardforgel rolled his eyes and shouted, "Benlos, you silly twit of a human girl!"

"Really?" Gabriella asked. "*Benlos* looks as though he's profited from this?"

All the fairies looked at Benlos, with his reminiscent-of-radishes clothing and his lumpy, bumpy cauliflower-like shoes.

Smiling sheepishly, Benlos shrugged, since there was obviously no comparison between what he was wearing and the gauzy, floaty attire of the others.

"Well," Ardforgel muttered, "so he hasn't used the teeth yet . . ."

"Then where are they?" Gabriella asked.

Benlos jumped to his feet, extending his arms out from his sides, an invitation to be searched. When none of the fairies responded, he patted his own arms, chest, and legs. He ran his fingers through his hair—which would have dislodged anything that might have been hidden there—and stretched his arms to reach as far around his back as he could around his wings. Nothing there, either. He was just unfastening the vine that held up his pants when Irate Fairy Woman ordered, "Enough."

"Obviously he doesn't have them on his person anymore," Ardforgel admitted grumblingly.

Now *Parf* jumped to *his* feet. "He didn't pass them on to me, neither," he said, and to demonstrate he began to repeat the same slapping-his-own-limbs motions of his father. "Gabby?"

As her nightgown was longer and looser than fairy clothing, Gabriella was thinking that proving she wasn't hiding anything might be difficult. So she was relieved when Irate Fairy Woman repeated—a bit more testily than before—"Enough!"

His arms folded defensively across his chest, Ardforgel pointed out, "He could have hidden them somewhere."

"I can attest that he hasn't been home in the last two days," Gabriella said. Seeing Ardforgel take a breath to protest, she added, "And, as an outsider—wrenched unwillingly from my own home—I have no reason to lie."

Ardforgel sat back to reconsider his options.

Gabriella asked, "And where, besides *his* own home, would be a safe place to hide such valuable items? Where other fairies would be unlikely to happen upon them and take them for their own?" This was not a compelling argument, Gabriella knew—but she didn't need to prove his innocence, just cast doubt about his guilt.

"You make a valid point, Changeling," Moderately Annoyed

Fairy Woman said. "But what reason would Councillor Ardforgel have to make up the story he told us?"

"You know him better than I do," Gabriella said. She quickly added, "And you know his wife. Is there any possibility of truth in what Benlos has said—that Ardforgel and Sylvimit are spending their dragons' teeth at such a rate that they are apt to run out? Could Ardforgel be desperate enough to replenish their supply that he was willing to believe the fanciful folktale Benlos told of a magic cauldron?"

"If he believed the story," said Close to Napping Fairy Man, who finally seemed wide awake, "why turn on Benlos before Benlos had a chance to work the cauldron's supposed magic?"

"That's a good point," Gabriella admitted. She didn't dare take too long to think of an answer for fear of losing the momentum she had gained. For the first time, all the members of the Council appeared receptive to human reason and open to the *possibility* of Benlos's innocence. Except, of course, for Ardforgel: *He* looked nervous. "A very good point." Gabriella licked her lips, hoping this didn't make her look as uncertain and shifty as Ardforgel did. So she hastened to say, "The answer is clear."

Well, not exactly.

She forced a laugh. "Though *clear* and *clearly* have . . . um . . . clearly . . . been overused words today." While nobody pointed out that *clearly* she was stalling for time, nobody smiled at her little wordplay, either.

She glanced at Benlos, but there was no help from him, as he watched her in apparent expectation that she knew what she was doing. She glanced at Parf . . .

141

. . . and suddenly the answer *was* clear.

She asked, "Parf, why are we here?"

Miserably—he definitely wasn't so certain of her talents as his father was—Parf admitted, "I haven't a clue."

"Yes, you do."

He gave her a don't-you-be-playing-your-word-games-with-me look.

"Who told us your father was appearing before the Council? That he was in trouble?"

As though suspecting a trap, Parf muttered, "Aunt Vimit."

"And how did she know?" Gabriella asked. She was watching Ardforgel and saw she was on the right track, even though Parf replied, "Dunno. Vomit knows everything and likes to tell everybody everything."

But Ardforgel was squirming.

More to the Council than to Parf, Gabriella asked, "Could she have come home and found the one dragon's tooth was gone? Could Ardforgel have admitted he'd given it to Benlos, and why? Could your aunt Vimit have been the one to point out that this cauldron plan could not possibly work, and that the only way to get back the tooth was to accuse Benlos of stealing it?"

"No," Ardforgel protested, but weakly. "Sylvimit wouldn't bring charges against Benlos over one tooth."

Gabriella reconsidered quickly. "But would she accuse him if there were fewer teeth than she expected there to be—because she has been spending them so freely, and you didn't want to admit you were running short, didn't want to tell her that both of you needed to be more frugal?"

142

Ardforgel's gaze took in the Council members. Gabriella was sure his lips were about to form the word *maybe*, but he shifted to, "You have no proof."

"Which," Gabriella pointed out, "is hardly the same as no."

"No," Ardforgel said, though it was—very clearly—too late.

Irate Fairy Woman slammed her hand against the table to get everyone's attention. "Serious questions have been raised," she declared. "This hearing will reconvene tomorrow and we can declare our official verdict then."

"But—" Ardforgel started.

"Tomorrow!" Irate Fairy Woman repeated.

And Gabriella even dared to hope the Councilwoman sounded impatient with him.

It was a start.

PHLEG

Fortunately, the search party that was looking for them was stumbling and bumbling through the woods, making enough noise that both Phleg and the bear heard them coming long before anybody was close enough to see or be seen. Fred was busy yawning, and so didn't notice.

"Thank you," Phleg told the bear.

The bear growled what was so clearly a *You're welcome, and thanks for all the stories* that Phleg was sure even someone who didn't speak bear would understand.

But . . . apparently there was *clear* and then there was *clear*.

Fred had seemed, if not comfortable with the situation, then at least willing to accept the idea of all three of them resting against the tree trunk. But now he suddenly paled. He scrambled back, as though trying to reverse himself through the trunk and out the other side.

The bear stood on its hind legs, momentarily looming over Fred—which was no more than polite leave-taking manners in bear society. But perceiving how nervous this made Fred, the bear considerately dropped to all fours and shambled off into the woods without another word.

"Whew!" Fred said. "That was a close call!" He saw the look Phleg was giving him. "Ooorrrr . . . maybe not?"

"Not," Phleg corrected him.

Fred's head drooped, and Phleg realized he was embarrassed. And ashamed. Both at having been afraid, especially unnecessarily so, and at proving yet again that he did not know as much about the world—at least the wilderness world—as she did.

So she fibbed, saying, "But it was a natural mistake." And she gave an encouraging nod and smile.

Fred smiled back—but while Phleg was still enjoying that, Fred at last became aware of the ruckus being made by the oncoming humans tromping through the woods toward them. "Hey!" he told Phleg as though he was breaking the news to her. "Listen! I think we're about to be rescued!"

Phleg was tempted to say *Not!* to that, too.

She did not need rescuing. *She* was tempted to run off after the bear, leaving the humans to sort things out. After all, nothing had changed since yesterday, when she had decided her only option was to run away. *She* was only here for one more day, because she was not the real Princess Gabriella, however much Fred might think she was.

It was no use growing fond of him.

But running, she realized, could put the bear in danger, if the rescue party chased after her.

And ... it would mean saying *good-bye* to Fred, whom she would probably never see again. Even if she had no business liking him, she would find that final good-bye difficult, so she preferred to put off saying it.

"Over here!" Fred called out to their rescuers, waving his arms, though surely the searchers could hear him long before they would see him.

Phleg didn't recognize the people from the castle, though they recognized her—or rather, they recognized Princess Gabriella. And they seemed more relieved to have found her than to see Prince Fred. Probably, Phleg thought, because the princess was likely to be even more inept in the forest than Fred.

It was a scary thought.

"I'm fine," she assured them several times as they hovered and twittered over her like anxious robin parents. The three men had each brought fur-lined cloaks for her, presumably in case they should not find her until the dead of winter, which was only—what?—five months away. (And how many cloaks could one princess have, anyway?) Two of the men proceeded to bundle her up against the chill of the summer afternoon, and the third was simply waiting for the other two to get out of his way. All this concern, she thought, and they didn't even know that she and Fred had been in the stream, as the sun, mercifully, had dried their clothing.

"Enough!" Phleg said, squirming out from beneath the heavy cloaks. "You're going to kill me with heat stroke! I'm totally unharmed. Prince Fred, however, *is* injured and needs to be helped back to the castle. Why don't you use the cloaks as a sort of sling to carry him?" She layered all three cloaks on top of one another for added strength and positioned one man at the end with the neck openings and the other two at the spread-out hems.

As they settled him on the not-quite-a-litter sling, Fred told the men, "Princess Gabriella has been amazing! She found me when I was lost, pulled me from the stream, and tended my injuries."

All of the men looked at Phleg in varying degrees of dumbfoundedness that grew with each of Gabriella's stated accomplishments. "Really?" one of them said, in the tone that polite people use instead of saying *You liar, you!*

Phleg realized that such deeds would have been beyond the real Gabriella. If the men believed Fred, she worried they might start to have doubts about *her*.

But, meanwhile, Fred was in no condition to recognize the nuances of skepticism. He nodded. "Not only that," he continued, "but she can talk to animals."

"Well," Phleg murmured, eager to deflect suspicion, "anybody can *talk* to animals."

"But they can understand her!" Fred insisted. "And she can understand them! She got a bullfinch, and a pair of beavers, and a bear to help me."

Phleg made sure she was standing where Fred couldn't see her as she tapped her head to indicate to the men that there was something wrong with Fred's thinking. "Prince Fred might have a fever," she informed them.

"Ah!" they said as they hefted him up on the litter and started back toward the castle. And they even periodically said, "Yes" and "Of course" and "Imagine that" as Fred chattered on and on about beavers and their yearlong busy season, and bears who liked stories . . .

Chapter 8

Evening

PRINCESS GABRIELLA

Gabriella was amazed that the Council didn't hold Benlos in captivity. They said he could go home or not as he wished, so long as he was back in the morning to hear their judgment.

"Surely that's a good sign," Gabriella observed to Parf after she, he, and Benlos stepped through the doorway and found themselves back in the Everywhere Room. "It must mean they trust him."

Benlos smiled and said, "Indeed."

But Parf was making a face that indicated Gabriella was wearisome. "*Or*," Parf said, "it might have something to do with the fact that the Council have all linked with him, so they'll know when he's using magic, and for exactly what spells." At her puzzled expression he explained, "It's like a leash. Like you use to lead your animals around."

"I don't personally have any animals," Gabriella reminded him.

Parf shrugged. He turned to his father. "Are you coming home with us? Or are you off on more of your travels?"

148

"Of course I'm coming home," Benlos said evenly, refusing to rise to Parf's bait.

Gabriella had no idea why Parf was in such a foul mood, but in any case it was a barely-speaking-to-each-other trio who stepped through another doorway out of the Everywhere Room . . . and into the yard in front of the little round house in the woods.

One or two of the younger children happened to be outside. "Daddy! Daddy!" they cried. "Daddy's home!"

The rest of the family came tumbling out of the house or from around the back.

Benlos swept up the youngest boy. "I'm so happy to see you!" he told the child. "Which one are you again?"

By the gleeful way the child announced his name, Gabriella could tell this was a regular game with them.

"My! There's an awful lot of you!" Benlos said as the children clamored for attention, even Daisy, who was next oldest after Phleg and Parf. "Just how many of you are there? Thirty-seven? Thirty-eight?"

"Twelve!" they corrected with squeals and laughter.

Gabriella found herself . . . well, she had been warned Benlos was charming, and she knew she should not be swayed by smiles and an easy manner. But she couldn't help but be won over by his relationship with the children. Still, at the same time her heart ached for missing her own father.

And then Mumsy came out, not rushing, wiping her hands on a rose petal towel. "Come back, have you?" she greeted her husband.

149

"Ahhh!" Benlos said. "And there's the light of my life, my bride, looking as young and beautiful as the day we met."

Mumsy snorted. But when Benlos touched the dragon's tooth necklace and a bouquet of wildflowers appeared in his hand, she accepted them from him.

"Waste of a good spell," she chided even as she buried her nose in the blooms. "If we wanted flowers, we could have picked them."

"But I picked these *for* you," Benlos told her. "And these for the children . . ." He held his arms out, and toys cascaded from his empty hands onto the lawn: whirligigs, and hoops, and dolls.

Mumsy looked up in alarm. "What have you done?" she demanded as the fairy children rushed forward with eager cries of anticipation to sort through the toys. "Where have you gotten that dragon's tooth?"

"Ardforgel," Benlos said. "And, no, this is not one of the ones in contention."

"You have more?" Mumsy asked in horror. "And things haven't been settled? You're still in trouble with the Council?"

"Not to worry, not to worry," Benlos assured her. "Parf and Gabby did an excellent job of defending me."

"So it *is* settled?" Mumsy asked, not sounding convinced.

"Well . . ."

Mumsy turned to Parf and Gabriella. "Can I get a straight answer from either of you?"

Since Parf was sulking, Gabriella answered, "The Council needs more time to decide, but it's looking—"

"Fabulous!" Benlos interjected.

"Hopeful," Gabriella countered.

Parf snorted.

Benlos once more touched the dragon's tooth locket, and Mumsy's bedraggled dress—originally an elm leaf, Gabriella suspected—suddenly became a sparkly lilac confection such as worn by the other fairy ladies Gabriella had seen.

"Oh my!" Mumsy said.

Several of the children looked up from the new toys. "Mumsy, you're beautiful!"

"Thank you," Mumsy said. "But, Benlos, this is too extravagant. Where am I ever going to wear this? Into the woods to take care of the animals?"

"No," Benlos said, taking her into his arms, "to dance with me under the moonlight."

Music came out of nowhere, reminiscent of handbells, soft and slow and beautiful.

It being only afternoon, there was no moonlight; but Benlos began to dance with Mumsy, and—after a moment of resistance—she gave in.

Gabriella felt a tingly sensation on her skin, and she realized Benlos had given all the rest of them, including her, new clothes. Hers were not exactly what a princess would wear—being more gauzy milkmaid-ish—but it was better than the nightdress she'd been wearing for two days now. Parf, too, had a new set of clothes, though that did nothing to soften the sourness of his expression.

The fairy children, in honor of their new clothing, began to chase one another around the yard.

"This is ridiculous," Parf grumbled.

"Mmmm," Mumsy said, her eyes closed, her cheek against Benlos's chest. Her feet had left the ground, supported by her fluttering wings and her husband's embrace.

Parf continued to complain. "You've got a brand-new powerful dragon's tooth, and you're using it on frivolous things. Has it ever occurred to you to save your wishes for some other day?"

"Today I have the tooth," Benlos said. "Who knows what some other day might bring?"

Behind the expanse of lawn where he and Mumsy danced, the house shimmered and grew larger, brighter. There was a porch now, and a fine table, laden with bowls and platters of food.

Gabriella asked, "Speaking of other days, shouldn't we be doing something to prepare for tomorrow?"

"What . . . specifically?" Benlos asked dreamily, swaying to the music with Mumsy in his arms. He also had begun to hover just above the ground.

"I don't know." *She* was the princess, but *he* was supposed to be the adult. Exasperated, Gabriella said, "Investigating . . . looking for witnesses . . . preparing statements . . ."

When his father didn't answer, Parf said, "You always do this. You're gone forever, then you breeze back in for a little bit, then you're gone again. Why do you keep leaving? What are you looking for? What's more important than us?"

"Nothing's more important than you." Benlos extracted his hand from Mumsy's long enough to pull a book out from under his shirt.

So much for patting himself down during the Council hearing, to prove he didn't have Ardforgel's dragons' teeth hidden on his person.

Parf's look was contemptuous. "That's human stuff." Parf used the same tone one would to say, *That's a BIG pile some horse left behind.* "What's that good for?"

"There's stories inside," Benlos said.

Parf wouldn't take the book, so Gabriella did, and Benlos resumed dancing.

Interested despite himself, Parf put his ear to the cover. "I don't hear no stories."

Gabriella opened the book to show Parf the words and the beautiful pictures.

"I don't understand," he said.

She explained, "The words are written down so people can remember the stories."

Parf snorted. "The stories can't be much good if writing down is the only way people can remember them."

Gabriella sighed. "You don't understand."

Parf gave her a scornful look. "That's what I just said." To his father, he repeated, "This is human stuff. Fit for humans, maybe, like Princess Gabby." He turned away from all of them and stomped into the house.

"I like stories," Benlos said, soft and disappointed to Parf's retreating back. Then he looked at Gabriella and mused, "Gabby *is* rather a different name for a princess."

Gabriella nodded in agreement. "My name is really Gabriella." She gave a proper curtsey, despite the milkmaid outfit. "Gabby sounds more like a misbehaving dog. Or an eighty-seven-year-old woman who sits in the town square and gossips all day."

"No," Benlos said. "That wasn't what I was thinking. I was thinking it was nice. A pet name. For a person, not a pet. A term of endearment."

"But nobody calls me that except for Parf," Gabriella said.

"Ah!" Benlos said, and after that he gave himself over to dancing with Mumsy.

PHLEG

The rescue party ran into a pair of men who were also searching for the lost princess. They were but a short distance from the castle now, evidenced by the fact that the trees were getting more spread apart, and the castle's spires could occasionally be glimpsed above the branches.

"Yay!" these new men said.

"You've found the princess!"

"Well met, Princess."

Then they turned their attention to those guards who were carrying the sling fashioned from Gabriella's cloaks, and the injured Fred within it. "Here, let us help with that."

But the three men who had carried Fred so far refused to give him up now. "No. I've got it," one of them said.

"Nope. Doing fine," said the second.

"All set here," said the third.

Phleg didn't understand this. If someone ever offered to take over a task from her, she would have gladly accepted. She was always in favor of someone doing her work for her. She wondered if she could ask them to carry *her*, as she was getting a bit weary. Was that something princesses were likely to ask for? But all three of the cloaks were being used to transport Fred, and she didn't want to be carried back to the castle like a sack of turnips slung over someone's shoulder. People really *should* have wings—they were a big help for tired feet. She was about to ask the men—*if* they were to carry her, how they'd go about doing so. But before she had a chance, the newcomers said, "All right. Good-bye, then."

They turned abruptly and headed back the way they'd just come. Their steps went from a brisk pace, getting faster and faster, till they were out-and-out running. They were also shoving one another, each trying to take the lead, before they disappeared among the trees.

Phleg considered, but then had to ask, "What's that all about, then?"

The man who had said he was doing fine paused to readjust his hold on the edge of the cloaks. "Each wants to be the one to announce you've been found. First to report where you are might get a reward."

In a very short while, they heard the sound of trumpets, proving that one or another of the men had delivered the news and that help was on the way.

The fanfares got closer and closer, and Phleg suggested, "Why don't you stop walking and rest, since help is on its way? They can't very well *not* find us at this point."

155

Well, *probably* not. It seemed difficult to underestimate humans.

"No, no," the three rescuers said, forcing hearty smiles despite the throbbing veins in their necks and the sweat on their faces. Apparently they wanted to be seen working. Phleg guessed they were hoping there might be a reward for that, too.

In another moment, a party from the castle appeared, led by the two kings—Gabriella's father, King Humphrey, and Fred's, King Leopold—along with a whole retinue of other men, including trumpet players.

"Gabriella!" King Humphrey cried, his arms wide as he rushed toward Phleg.

Phleg instinctively looked over her shoulder. How had the princess made it back without the changeling spell reversing? Then she realized he meant her.

Drat! And she hadn't determined yet whether royal people called their fathers *Father* or *Daddy*.

She settled for saying, "I'm so glad to see you!" and she enveloped the king in a tight hug that seemed to take him by surprise, or at least took the breath out of him. But then he hugged her back and said, "We've been so worried about you. Why did you run away?"

"Well . . . ," Phleg said. "It seemed the thing to do at the time."

Apparently he was too pleased at having his daughter back to press, and meanwhile King Leopold had made it to Fred's side. "Hello, Father," Fred said, a bit hazily, probably because of the leaves she'd had him chew for the pain.

Father, Phleg thought. Finally an answer to her father/daddy/ papa dilemma. *You couldn't have helped me out with that before, Fred?*

156

"What's the matter with him?" Leopold demanded.

"He hurt his leg," chorused all three of the men who had carried him. Apparently, despite scoffing at the two who had raced to be first to bring word to the castle, these men were also eager to share news.

"Gabriella has been taking care of me," Fred announced, slurring his words a little. He gave Phleg's hand a squeeze. Except, of course, that she was no longer in hand-squeezing distance, having stepped away to embrace her—*Gabriella's*—father. Fred held his hand up in front of his face and looked at both sides of it, as though hoping to find her hand there someplace. Still puzzled, he announced, "She has been a wonder!"

"Then why are you talking funny?" his father demanded.

"Valerian leaves for the pain," Phleg told him. "Once we get back to the castle"—she couldn't say *home*, and hoped nobody would notice—"you should make up some yarrow for him. Brew some rosemary tea. Maybe betony."

"I should, should I?" Leopold thundered. Did the man always thunder everything?

"Well, yes," Phleg said. Didn't he want his son to get better?

"I think," said one of the three men who had been helping them, "she means *you* in a general way, sire, as in *your attendants.* Or," he offered generously, "one of ours. We have both a physician and a wisewoman."

While the king mulled over that clarification, one of the others added, "Princess Gabriella has been instrumental in finding Prince Frederic, in rescuing him from . . ." He trailed off. Understandably, they weren't clear on exactly what had

157

happened. Ever since they'd found the pair, Fred's speech had been bizarrely full of accounts of forest wildlife, even before the princess had found the leaves for him to chew on. And *she* hadn't been forthcoming with helpful information, either. "Well, she found him injured and rescued him, and tended him, and has been very brave and resourceful."

Gabriella's father gave her shoulders a squeeze. "Well done!" he said proudly.

The third man, with nothing new left to report, chimed in, "Yes indeedy."

"And I love her," Fred announced.

Which both filled Phleg's heart with song and made it sink. He loved Gabriella, not her.

The three members of their rescue party gave a spontaneous cheer. The newcomers who had accompanied the kings were a bit more reserved, but most smiled and nodded. King Humphrey, however, looked to his daughter for her reaction. When he saw her staring at her feet without responding, he gave her another squeeze.

King Leopold, of course, was the least enthusiastic. He made throat-clearing noises that sounded like he had a chipmunk caught halfway down. Patting Fred's head awkwardly, he bent closer, but his voice carried. "There's something a bit off about that girl, you mark my words. This is an important alliance, and we can't risk—"

Fred struggled and managed to sit up. Speaking more clearly than anything he'd said in a while, he repeated, loud and strong, "I love her."

158

Leopold made some more harrumphing sounds, then told Fred, "We'll see."

By then, some of the men who had been lingering at the back of the kings' arrival party stepped forward, leading horses. "We have the supplies to make a proper litter for Prince Frederic," one of them said, "and we can have him home in a trice. Meanwhile, the horses can make the journey in no time."

"Well, good for the horses," Phleg said, wondering why the man chose now to share this useless information. But then she realized he meant the horses would *carry* the rest of them. People used animals, she reminded herself.

Leopold was giving her a squinty-eyed look.

"I mean," she amended, "that if I rode on the horse, then I wouldn't be able to be with Fr—Prince Fred. Rick." She escaped King Humphrey's embrace and stood by Fred, grabbing hold of his hand again.

"My hero," he whispered in a tone that could only be described as gooey. And still loudly enough for everyone to hear.

"I must insist," King Humphrey said. "We are leaving Prince Frederic in capable hands, and your mother is most anxious to see you."

Phleg remembered seeing the queen take a spill while running after *her*. Gabriella's mother had been kind, and Phleg hoped she hadn't injured herself.

Two of the men approached, leading a pair of horses.

Now what?

Before she could stop him, one of the men put his hands around her waist and lifted her up onto the back of the horse.

Phleg gave a sharp squeal of dismay. "I can't!" she said, waving her arms so that the man would lift her off. She *really* missed her wings.

"Take hold—"

"I can't!" she repeated. "Take me off, *take me off*, TAKE ME OFF!"

The man took her off, but she suspected that had less to do with her commanding him to do so than the fact that the horse was beginning to get wide-eyed at her noise and flailing hands.

Everyone was looking at her.

"I can't ride a horse," she said.

"Why not?" King Humphrey asked. To King Leopold, he added, "She's a most excellent horsewoman."

"Yay for you!" Fred called. "She's most excellent at everything."

Phleg suspected she could no longer blame the bump on her head that she'd gotten the previous morning. If people hadn't forgotten about that incident entirely, they would think the crack on her head had made her an imbecile. "I'm too tired," she said. "I've slept outside and been walking all day..." She wasn't helping things, she could tell.

"All the more reason to ride," King Humphrey said.

"I'm too tired to hold on properly," Phleg explained—assuming that humans must have to hold on to horses.

"You poor dear." Gabriella's father gave her another hug and kissed her on the forehead. "Then you shall ride with me, as you did when you were a little child."

"Oh," Phleg said. "Really... I don't..."

And so the king mounted first, then—before she even had a chance to ask the horse for permission—a man lifted her up into the seat-thing that was on the horse's back, and Gabriella's father took the leash things that trailed from the horse's mouth, circling his arms around her.

It was a comforting, safe feeling.

Until the horse began to move.

"I think my balance is off," she said. "From being tired."

"I'll hold on to you," he assured her.

And he did, all the way back to the castle, where big brass bells pealed to greet them as soon as they came in sight. He even carried her inside—not exactly like a bag of turnips.

But he didn't bring her back to her own room; he brought her to the queen's chamber. Both queens—Gabriella's mother and Fred's—sat there, each holding on her lap a big round hoop with fabric stretched over it. They didn't seem to be doing any sewing, however. Instead, they were talking quietly together.

Gabriella's mother gave a very unqueenly squeal of joy at seeing her. Both women, Phleg could see, were red around the rims of their eyes and a bit splotchy-faced. Gabriella's mother stood, though she had one foot in a bucket—presumably cold water to lessen swelling. Fred's mother made her sit back down, or she would certainly have rushed forward despite her injury.

"Princess Gabriella is fine," the king announced hastily to both women. "Prince Frederic is slightly the worse for wear, but—really—his injuries are minor and are being attended to. He should be back in fine fettle soon. He's in jovial humor and is being taken to his room even as we speak."

Fred's mother rose and kissed Phleg, first on one cheek, then the other. Perhaps she worried that her lips had missed the mark with the first.

"Thank you," Fred's mother said to the king, her eyes filling with fresh tears, which seemed silly, since she'd just heard Fred was being returned to her mostly unharmed. Phleg wondered if maybe she distrusted the king's report and thought he'd just said what he'd said to get her to leave.

Before Phleg could work it out, the queen hurried out of the room. Which left only Gabriella's mother. Still sitting, she held her arms wide for Phleg, her fingers twitching as though eager to hold her daughter. "Oh, Gabriella," she said, and she was crying, too, though as far as she knew Gabriella was home safe and sound, and the time for crying was past. *I'll never understand humans*, Phleg thought.

But the king set Phleg on her feet, and Phleg went to the queen, who gave her a hug. It was a nice hug. Mumsy's hugs were few and far between, and not so well padded.

"Are you all right? Are you truly all right?"

Phleg nodded.

"What happened? Why in the world did you ever run off like that?"

Phleg couldn't think what to say, so she said, "I don't want to talk about it."

And, amazingly, the queen declared, "Well, then, we shan't. And we shall spend a nice quiet evening, just the three of us, to celebrate your safe return to us. Have supper brought here to us rather than in the din of the dining hall." She patted the

162

cushion beside her, which Fred's mother had just vacated. She seemed reluctant to let go of Phleg's hand, and all the while Gabriella's father continued beaming at them.

Feeling a wicked imposter, Phleg grew uncomfortable. Eventually—though feeling guilty both for doing it and for not doing it sooner—she extracted her hand.

The queen smiled at her. "Shall I send for Ellen to bring your embroidery to you?"

Embroidery. That must be the fabric stretched over the hoop. "I'm a bit tired," Phleg said. "How about if I just watch you?"

And she did, and she was amazed at the delicate little rosebuds that the queen created with different strands of pinks and reds, and she thought—though it was a ridiculous thought—that she wouldn't mind someone teaching her how to do that.

At one point in the evening, the princess's friend Amanda poked her head in the room. "I don't know what's going on with you," she said. "But I'm glad you're safely home."

Phleg considered carefully. "I'm glad *you're* safely home, too," she said. How could anyone argue with that?

Amanda didn't argue. But she didn't stay, either.

Which was probably all for the best.

And neither the king nor the queen pressed her for answers, and eventually Phleg fell asleep with her head on the queen's shoulder.

~ *Chapter* 9 ~

Liars

PRINCESS GABRIELLA
❧

The dragon's tooth ran out of magic just as Benlos put the finishing touches on the breakfast feast, so the second bowl of strawberries was a bit skimpy. But only compared to the first huge, overflowing bowl.

Gabriella was just pleased that no one had to prepare the meal, just as no one had to prepare or clean up yesterday evening. Dishes that materialized full of food and dissolved once you were through with them struck her as an idea that could easily catch on.

"You could at least have saved some magic so we wouldn't have to walk all the way to the Council," Parf complained.

Mumsy smacked him on the back of the head—not hard enough to hurt, Gabriella surmised, just enough to get his attention.

"Easy come, easy go," Benlos pointed out.

"Go!" echoed Miss-mot. She was sitting on her father's lap, and she nodded so vigorously that the bow in her hair came loose and fell into her father's porridge bowl.

"You could try taking this seriously, you know," Parf grumbled.

"I am," Benlos insisted, but since he was spooning the ribbon out of the porridge as he said it, Gabriella felt there was no being sure *what* he was declaring he took seriously: appearing before the Council or removing hair ornaments from his breakfast.

"Still," Gabriella said, thinking to deflect Parf's bad mood by getting him to consider whether the sudden depletion of the tooth might have caught his father unaware, "can one *feel* the magic running out?"

"Oh yes," said all the fairies—adults and children. Even Miss-mot joined in after everyone else, though Gabriella suspected she had no idea to what she was saying yes. The fairy toddler seemed fully occupied in eating her father's porridge with both hands.

"And yet . . ." Gabriella gave a cheerful smile. "It's a perfect day for a walk."

"Except," Parf pointed out, "the Council is nearly a day's walk from here."

Not good news, since Benlos had been ordered to return that morning.

Did this make him a fugitive?

It was hard to find something cheerful to say about being a fugitive.

"Not to worry," Benlos told her and any other family members who might need reassuring. "Parf tends toward drama and tumult. For one thing, the walk is closer to half a day's journey, not a full day. More importantly, the Council wouldn't be willing to wait that long. Don't forget they've established a magic link to monitor where I am and what magic I've been using. They, too, will have been aware of the waning of the tooth. So when I don't show up, they'll catch on that there's no way for me to get there in anything resembling a timely fashion. Being the resourceful, not to mention impatient, fairies they are—they'll expend their magic to fetch me."

Surely that wasn't the way to create a good impression.

"I see," Gabriella said. Benlos seemed determined not to allow concern about *anything* to mar his good humor. She herself had tossed and turned all night long, trying to figure out a way to prove Benlos's innocence. All her restlessness and stomach-churning anxiety had been for nothing: No ideas had come to her. Which put her no further ahead than the never-worry-about-anything Benlos, who looked both well rested and jovial.

Gabriella stole a glance at Parf as he shoveled food into his mouth, not talking with his siblings. By the circles under his eyes, she suspected that he, too, was giving more thought to his father's future than his father was doing. Certainly more than he was willing to let anyone know about.

To change the subject—to get Parf away from thinking how infuriating his father was—she asked, "So what happens to the dragon's tooth now that it's used up? Or has it physically worn away to nothing?"

Parf snorted.

"Not at all." Benlos shook the tooth out of the locket he wore around his neck.

Miss-mot made a grab for the tooth, but Benlos curled his fingers around it while using his other hand to distract her with a strawberry.

Which made Gabriella ask, "Are used teeth dangerous?"

"Only if little ones try to swallow them," Mumsy said.

Benlos handed it to Gabriella.

Sitting in the palm of her hand, it looked . . . unremarkable. It was about as long as her little finger and no wider, but it came to a sharp point. *Baby tooth*, she reminded herself. "What do you do with used-up teeth?"

"Use them to poke your sisters," one of the fairy boys said, giggling and demonstrating on his closest neighbor with his finger.

"Decoration for your dress," one of the girls said.

"Scratch in the dirt."

"Scratch an itch on your back."

"Splint for an injured bird's wing."

"Anything you can use a short stick for."

Such a small thing to be the source of so much trouble.

Seeing her studying the tooth, Benlos told Gabriella, "You can keep it if you want."

Miss-mot made another grab for it, this time more successfully. Gabriella used one hand to tickle, the other to open the child's syrup-sticky fingers. She set the tooth beyond Miss-mot's reach in a basket-shaped dish somewhere between a saucer and a bowl that must be for discarded strawberry tops. What use, she wondered, could a human princess find for a dragon's tooth?

Parf reached around Daisy to get at the syrup. Not counting Miss-mot, who could be excused because of her age, the other children were mostly remembering to ask for things to be passed. "Mumsy's is better," he mumbled around a mouthful of porridge. He probably meant it as a complaint against the food his father had magicked rather than as a compliment for Mumsy, but Mumsy smiled and said, "Thank you, dear."

Parf stopped talking and concentrated on looking disagreeable.

With a nod to his eldest son, Benlos asked, "Will the two of you accompany me again?"

Parf snorted.

Gabriella asked, "Will the Council know to bring us, too?"

"We must hold hands," Benlos explained.

"I ain't holding hands with nobody," Parf said from across the table.

But he was the only one who seemed unwilling to accompany Benlos. "Me, too! Me, too!" the rest of the children clamored, getting out of their chairs and surrounding their father, several clutching at his clothing with sticky hands.

"Oh," Benlos said, "I wish I could bring you, my lovelies. But children as precious as you are not allowed in the Council room, for then the councillors could not concentrate and they would all be going . . ." Benlos scratched the top of his head, all the while making a very vacant expression, and his speech became a simpleton's drawl. "'What new senseless rule was that we were going to enact? These children are too precious, and now I can't remember.' And then where would we be without that new senseless rule?"

The children all laughed and cheered.

"Sit down, children," Mumsy said, "and finish eating. And let your father finish eating."

"Too late." Benlos suddenly handed Miss-mot over to the child on his right. Gabriella could see that the fairy father was growing wispy and a bit see-through. He put his hand over Gabriella's on the tabletop. "And here we go . . . ," he said. "Parf?"

Parf sat back with his arms folded across his chest.

But at the last moment and with a sigh of exasperation, Parf slammed his open palm over their clasped hands.

Gabriella tightened her free hand around the tiny bowl that held the dragon's tooth. It wasn't that she had a *good* plan . . . but a thought that might eventually grow into a plan was beginning to flit about her mind.

There was a slight tingliness, and she guessed she herself was becoming wispy and see-through . . .

Then they were once more standing before the Council.

"You are late," Irate Fairy Woman informed Benlos irately.

"I *do* apologize." Benlos let go of his grip on Gabriella and Parf so that he could place his hand directly over his heart.

"Be that as it may," she muttered, no doubt guessing she'd get no better an answer from him, but unable to let him have the last word.

Moderately Annoyed Fairy Woman looked . . . well, she still looked moderately annoyed. But Close to Napping Fairy Man seemed a bit better rested and more alert this morning. Gabriella supposed that meant she had to switch to thinking of him as Council Fairy Man.

Ardforgel . . . Ardforgel looked as though *he*, too, had spent a sleepless night.

Good, Gabriella thought. *That's what a guilty conscience will do to you.*

169

Parf leaned his head close to Gabriella's as he got one of the extra chairs into place at the table. Whispering, he asked her, with a glance toward his father, "Know why he wanted us here?"

She shook her head.

"So we can break the news to Mumsy and them, once Council decrees he's not coming back."

"That's—you don't know that's going to happen."

He shrugged and would have left her to fetch her own chair, but his father stepped in and pulled one to the table for her.

Irate Fairy Woman folded her hands before her. She spoke in a calm and not unkind tone. "The Council has looked into Councillor Ardforgel's finances; in this, Councillor Ardforgel has been cooperative."

Gabriella glanced at Ardforgel's drawn face and thought, *Maybe cooperative, but surely not happy.*

"We have also looked into woods-fairy Benlos's finances."

"Such as they are," Benlos said.

"Such as they are," Irate Fairy Woman agreed. "In addition, we have talked to friends and family members of both of you—"

"Which?" Gabriella blurted out. And when no one told her to silence herself, she added, "Family members?" And, seeing that she still hadn't been escorted from the room, she tacked on, "Since no one came and spoke to us?"

Moderately Annoyed Fairy Woman said, "Obviously immediate family members, those most close of relations, would not have been summoned lest they be asked to present testimony that might be against their own interests."

"You were hearing testimony without our being present?" Gabriella asked. "That's . . . that's . . ."

"Perfectly acceptable procedure in Fairy Council proceedings," said Council Fairy Man. "Especially given that there were no surprises. And keep in mind that the stipulation against close relatives appearing prevented Sylvimit from speaking on Ardforgel's behalf as thoroughly as it prevented Luna from speaking for Benlos."

Gabriella nodded grudgingly. "Does Benlos get to know *which* friends and relatives were questioned?"

"No," said Irate Fairy Woman. "As I was saying, we have talked to friends and family members, speaking to them about the two of you, both in general terms and specific. *And*," she hastened to add, as though reading Gabriella's mind, "by *specific*, I mean that we spoke to some who were in attendance on the green while Benlos wove his fanciful story of magic cauldrons that could duplicate dragons' teeth."

Finally Benlos interrupted. "I never mentioned dragons' teeth during my story."

"A fact we already ascertained. Despite what your changeling might think, Benlos, we have not set our minds against you. You do, amazingly, have many friends."

Council Fairy Man said, "They lined up last night to speak on your behalf."

Benlos smiled.

Parf sat just the tiniest bit straighter, looking at his father with new appreciation.

171

"Right through the time for the evening meal," Council Fairy Man said. "*Your* friends on this side . . ." By the way he glanced at Ardforgel and fiddled with his lips and never finished that thought, Gabriella wondered whether Ardforgel had any friends to speak for him.

But of course he did. Pretending he didn't was just wishful thinking. A man with wealth—be that gold or dragons' teeth—always has friends.

Still, the way Council Fairy Man had spoken hinted that he recognized the difference.

"And yet," Irate Fairy Woman said, cutting through the hopeful feelings, "be *all* of that as it may, in the end this still comes down to the word of one fairy against another."

Gabriella jumped to her feet. "May I have the Council's indulgence?"

"We have been nothing *but* indulgent," Irate Fairy Woman snapped.

"Yes," Moderately Annoyed Fairy Woman answered Gabriella, "you may. In this one last instance."

Ardforgel sighed. Loudly.

Gabriella wished she'd had more time to work things out in her mind.

"Dragons' teeth," she said, "have a place in human tradition, too. Not that we can use them to create magic. But we recognize they have a magical quality. Even those teeth that have been—*apparently*—drained of their ability to grant fairy magic."

"Go on," Moderately Annoyed Fairy Woman said. "You're not doing a very good job of explaining."

Gabriella called to mind the bards who sometimes recited stories in the castle hall to help pass the long winter nights. She took a deep breath. "It is said," she told her audience, feeling that *It is said . . .* was almost as good a beginning to a story as *Once upon a time . . .* , "it is said that dragons do not lie. Do you have that same saying?"

In reality, as far as Gabriella knew, people did not normally converse with dragons, certainly not enough to have formed an opinion on their honesty. But in the pictures she had seen of dragons, they looked imposing and majestic—which she felt made them look trustworthy.

"Dragons are treacherous creatures," Irate Fairy Woman said—and that, Gabriella thought, was the end of that. Her plan, such as it was, had died before it could be born.

"But," Irate Fairy Woman continued, "they mislead by truths not spoken, by speaking in hints and generalities when that suits their purposes, or by citing a specific one-time reality that leads the listener to infer something that is false, all the while adhering to the truth in the strictest sense of the word."

"Dragons do not lie," Gabriella reiterated, hoping no one could see how relieved she was. "People do. Fairies do. Dragons do not."

"Your point?" Ardforgel snarled.

"It is said . . ." Satisfaction washed over Gabriella to see how repeating that phrase made Ardforgel squirm. "That once, during a human hearing much like today's, where one person said one thing and the other person said the opposite, the king who sat in judgment could not decide who was speaking the truth and who was lying."

"Let me guess," Ardforgel said. "He decided to believe the more unlikely of the two."

"Councillor Ardforgel," Irate Fairy Woman snapped, "if you keep interrupting, we'll never get to the end of this testimony."

"The king," Gabriella continued, "remembered that dragons do not lie. That dragons despise liars. So he sent for a dragon's tooth, and one was brought to him. He told the first man to hold the tooth tightly in his hand and to repeat what he already had said to the court. The man did. And nothing happened."

"A thrilling story," Ardforgel muttered, stifling a yawn. "Absolutely awe-inspiring."

"So then the king had the second man hold tight to the tooth and repeat what *he* had previously sworn to. The man started to speak, but suddenly yelped in surprise. And pain. 'Continue,' the king ordered. The man resumed speaking, but his face and his voice were tight with pain. Once more he stopped. He very clearly was trying to unclench his fist, but he could not. Then those in the court saw the man's hand was turning a purplish black. The unnatural and painful-looking color continued to spread, following the veins up the man's arm, till his arm was as dark and swollen as the hand. And then the man started to choke, and the onlookers could see the veins in his neck were beginning to throb and darken. And he coughed up blood and then fell over dead. All because the dragon's tooth would not permit him to speak lies after taking an oath to speak the truth."

The fairies looked from one to the other.

"Wow," Benlos said. "I never heard that story."

Gabriella wanted to kick him. Of course he hadn't heard that story before—she had just made it up. "Have you heard *every* human story?" she asked.

"Well, no," Benlos admitted.

"So I suggest," Gabriella hurried on, "that we have each of you—Ardforgel and Benlos—take a turn holding this dragon's tooth." She picked up the tiny dish that contained the tooth she had pried from Miss-mot's hand. She gave the dish a little shake, causing the tooth to rattle against the sides. "And we'll see if the tooth poisons one of you as a liar."

The two Fairy Councilwomen looked the most skeptical.

Ardforgel, she was convinced, looked the most nervous.

Benlos leaned forward and took the dragon's tooth.

Gabriella asked him to declare that what he was about to say was the full truth. He did, and then he repeated his version of the story, where the only tooth of Ardforgel's he had was the one Ardforgel had freely given him.

"Now Ardforgel's turn," Gabriella said.

"This is ridiculous," Ardforgel complained. "Such a story is pure fancifulness."

"Then no harm will come to you, just as no harm came to Benlos, and I will be proven a fool." She motioned for Benlos to return the tooth to the little plate, then pushed it toward

175

Ardforgel. "Take the tooth from the saucer," she instructed, "hold it in your clenched hand and declare your intention to speak the truth. Then tell us once again your version of what happened between you and Benlos. You must hold the tooth itself," Gabriella instructed, for it all came down to this, "tooth against skin."

"Yes, I got that," Ardforgel snarled. The very picture of irritation, he snatched at the shallow bowl.

Except instead of catching hold of the dish, his sudden movement sent it skittering across the table and clear off the edge.

"No harm done," he declared with admirable enthusiasm as he dove under the table to retrieve it. "I've got it."

Good thing: The Council members were too mindful of their dignity to bestir themselves. And both Parf and Benlos were looking at Gabriella with is-there-something-you're-expecting-us-to-be-doing? expressions.

She wasn't sure yet.

Ardforgel resurfaced quickly—with the empty bowl in one hand, and his other hand clenched into a fist.

Ha! Gabriella thought while he resettled himself, pulling his shirt straight and making sure his hair was still perfectly spiky. *Got you!*

"Your questions?" Ardforgel asked smugly, his aggravation apparently evaporated.

He thought *he* was fooling *her*. Working hard to keep her face from giving away her excitement, Gabriella asked, "Do you promise to tell the truth?"

"Yes," he snapped.

"Then begin now. And make sure you are scrupulously accurate. I should hate for the tooth to poison you because of a minor oversight." She smiled, perhaps indulging in a bit of unprincessly gloating.

Ardforgel repeated the story he had told the day before, of meeting Benlos and inviting him into his home, then of noticing—after Benlos left—that the door to the cabinet where he kept the extra dragons' teeth was ajar, and the dragons' teeth gone.

"Fine," Gabriella said, having to fight to keep her voice calm and even. "You're all right? No tingling in your hand? No odd sensation of any sort?"

Dig your own grave, she thought. As she'd hoped, he'd been too afraid to take the tooth. That was why he'd intentionally knocked the bowl to the floor—to rid it of the tooth. And now everyone would see.

Ardforgel said, "No. Dumb twit of a human girl. I, for one, have been telling the truth all along."

"Well then," she said, "open your hand. Show us the tooth."

They would see his hand was empty. And his fear of holding it while he spoke would show he was a liar.

Ardforgel placed his hand over his heart as though stricken. "I can't believe this," he said, "that my word should be questioned. That you would think I had made this up." He looked around at the Council, at each one of them in turn. "My heart aches—aches!—that you, my friends, should allow her to talk to me as though to a common criminal."

"Yeah, yeah," Parf said, "so cough up the tooth already."

For one moment Gabriella, looking at his self-satisfied countenance, wondered how he could continue to play at this when he was about to be found out.

And then he held his hand out, uncurled his fingers, and showed everyone the tooth. The tooth. In his hand, after all. Despite Gabriella's apparently-not-so-clever plan to have him reveal himself as a liar.

Smirking, Ardforgel let the tooth drop with an audible *clink!* back into the bowl.

"Well, that was certainly enlightening," he drawled. "Fine human tradition there. Your system of justice is exemplary." To the members of the Council he said, "Don't forget: You said that was the last time you would humor her."

"Except I'm not finished," Gabriella said. Even though she was. She just couldn't bring herself to admit it. She looked at Benlos, hoping something would come to her . . .

And something did.

Benlos, she saw, was wiping his right hand with his left thumb.

Gabriella asked him, "Did you feel anything while you held the tooth?"

"No tingling," he said.

For a smart fairy, he was being unaccommodating.

"What *did* you feel?" Gabriella insisted.

"Nothing," Benlos said. Even his wings drooped. "I'm sorry."

He was sorry? *He* was worried about disappointing *her*?

178

Gabriella held her own hand out, then touched her palm with the fingers of her other hand.

"Except," Benlos said, catching on to what she was asking, "it was sticky." He looked at the members of the Council. "My youngest daughter wanted to hold the tooth as we ate this morning. She got porridge and syrup on it."

"Ardforgel?" Gabriella asked.

He hesitated only a moment. "Yes," he agreed. "Sticky."

"Hold out your hands," Gabriella told both fairies.

Benlos showed his hands. His right palm was shiny with syrup.

Ardforgel said, "I wiped my hand on my trousers."

"Benlos," Gabriella said, "would you wipe your hand on your trousers?"

Benlos did, then once again held his palm upright. Now it had pieces of lint stuck to it.

Ardforgel said, "I . . . did a little cleansing spell."

"No, you didn't," said Moderately Annoyed Fairy Woman.

Council Fairy Man said, "We would have felt that."

"It was just a tiny spell." Ardforgel's voice was getting strident.

"Which," Irate Fairy Woman said, emphasizing each word, "we would have felt."

"It was more," Ardforgel told them, "like a wish that my hand was clean. I probably didn't even cause magic to happen. It was probably more the tiny lick I gave my hand while you were all paying attention to Benlos."

The Council members were all looking at Ardforgel in much the same way they had looked at Benlos the previous day.

179

"You saw I was holding the tooth!" Ardforgel said. He picked it up out of the bowl and held it up. "Most of the stickiness must have come off on Benlos's hand. I can repeat my testimony."

It was Parf who came to the rescue. He suddenly ducked under the table. "Aha!" he cried.

"What?" Irate Fairy Woman asked.

Parf didn't answer but only repeated, "Aha!" He was pointing at something beneath the table.

Everyone ducked their heads to look, the Council members no longer worried about their dignity.

And there, on the floor, was another dragon's tooth.

Irate Fairy Woman leaned way over and picked it up. A dust bunny had gotten stuck to it. With her other hand, she scooped up the dragon's tooth Ardforgel had been holding.

"*This* one," Irate Fairy Woman said, "this used-up old dragon's tooth, is sticky." She shook then blew on it, and still the dust bunny continued to cling to it. "This other one is not sticky. It is also not used up."

"You substituted one of your own," Council Fairy Man said. "You tossed away the tooth the changeling handed you while you distracted us by knocking over the bowl." He reached over and pulled Ardforgel's locket out from beneath his shirt, flipped it open, and revealed its emptiness. "Then, once you saw you needed to show you were holding a tooth, you pulled out the one you had in here."

"It was a stupid human test," Ardforgel protested.

"That you were afraid to take," said Moderately Annoyed Fairy Woman.

Irate Fairy Woman said, "Benlos, we will speak to you later."

And then Gabriella found herself once more in Mumsy's kitchen, with Parf and Benlos. The rest of the family had apparently finished breakfast, for the kitchen was tidy and empty.

"Was that true?" Parf asked.

"Was what true?" both Gabriella and Benlos asked.

Parf looked annoyed that he had to explain. "That humans use dragons' teeth to poison liars?"

"It was a story," Gabriella answered.

"Hmm," Parf said.

"It was a very good story," Benlos said. "Did you make it up yourself?"

"Yes and no," Gabriella said.

Parf threw his hands up in exasperation. "Oh, here we go!"

"I meant: I used what I had—the dragon's tooth—to remake an old folktale into a story that would fit the circumstances. The circumstances being that suspicion makes cowards of the guilty."

"More human logic," Parf said.

Gabriella shrugged.

Parf glanced at his father before mumbling to her, "But thank you."

PHLEG

❧⁘❧

Phleg woke up in the wonderful princess bed she had been in that first morning. Someone—either Gabriella's father or one

181

of the servants—must have carried her here. Someone—again, there was no telling who—had taken off her shoes, but she was still wearing the same intensely blue dress she'd been wearing since her morning in the garden, when she'd lain on her stomach behind the shrubbery, listening to Fred entertain his little brother with stories he made up. It was the same dress she'd been wearing when she fell into the moat, and ran into the woods, and spent the night there; the same dress she'd gone into the stream in, and sat next to a bear in, and ridden a horse in, and eaten a dinner in with the king and queen last night, when she'd been too tired to consistently get the food into her mouth.

She was aware that there was *something* in the room that didn't smell as nice as that other morning, and she suspected it was her.

There were twigs and leaves and a bit of algae on the pillow, evidently caught in her hair these last two days—another disadvantage to the long hair Princess Gabriella favored, beyond its sheer weight. When she sat up, something dug into Phleg's side. She fished out a piece of bark from the tree she and Fred and the bear had been leaning against while they awaited rescue. Phleg hadn't even been aware of the dress ripping. She supposed, considering how all of the princess's dresses looked just-made, that she would not be allowed to wear this dress again.

She wondered how Fred was doing and hoped a good night's rest had done as much for him as it had for her.

But then she saw that someone had placed a cup on the

little table beside the bed, and she got distracted from thinking about Fred by the sweet milk that Gabriella apparently drank every morning.

Could it really taste as good as she remembered?

Phleg reached for the cup, and managed not to fall out of the bed.

And, yes, the milk was every bit as wonderful as she remembered.

"Delicious," she said out loud—because it was *so* delicious it warranted her saying so.

Someone must have been listening by the door. There came the rapping of knuckles against the wood. Gabriella's servant, Ellen, came in. "Are we feeling better?" Ellen asked with what struck Phleg as an overabundance of cheer.

"Better than what?" Phleg asked. "Or who?" Was the question Ellen's way of indicating Fred was not doing well?

"Better than we were feeling yesterday," Ellen said. "Or . . . even the day before?"

Phleg had to pause to think this over. "Well," she finally said, considering that she felt rested and that she *hadn't* bumped her head this morning, "*I'm* feeling better. But there's no way for me to know if you are."

Ellen blinked a couple of times before saying, "I'm feeling better if you are."

"Well, I am," Phleg said.

"Then I am, too," Ellen told her.

"Well, now that that's settled," Phleg said, "I wonder if Fred— Prince Frederic—is feeling better."

"I am told he is much improved."

"Good." Phleg swung her legs off the bed. "Then I'd like to see him."

"First," Ellen said, more forcefully than was her custom, "a bath."

"For you, me, or Fred?"

"For you. I'm sure Prince Frederic has been attended to already."

"All right," Phleg agreed, because she could see there was no way Ellen was going to let her pass unless she *did* agree. "Is there a lake nearby, or will I bathe in the moat?"

Ellen sighed, but then she clapped her hands, which must have been a signal to more servants, who were apparently waiting in the hall.

Two came in bearing a huge metal container—more like a cooking cauldron than anything else Phleg could think of, but big enough to hold more stew than her family could eat in a month—and this they set on the floor.

Curious, Phleg looked inside. It was empty, which made sense because unless it was carrying a cloud it would have been too heavy for the servants to have lifted.

Phleg looked up in time to see a whole line of servants entering the room, each bearing a huge pitcher. Were those empty, too?

No, the servants poured water out of their pitchers into the container.

"Oh," Phleg said after the fourth or fifth servant, "you're bringing the lake to me." At least twice as many more were still waiting their turns.

"Mmm," Ellen said.

The last servant had a much smaller pitcher, and when she emptied this, the smell of lavender filled the room.

Ellen leaned over to put a hand in the water. "Feels just right," she declared as the other servants filed out. "Princess?"

"Um . . ." Phleg wondered if she was supposed to wear her clothes into this indoor lake the servants had provided. It would save time if she washed both herself and the dress, but she had already suspected that this particular dress would be judged no longer fit for a princess.

Ellen crooked her finger. Phleg approached and let the servant help her out of her clothes and into the warm, fragrant water. Ellen took charge of washing Phleg's hair, which was a good thing because Phleg wouldn't have known where to start with hair that long.

Eventually both hair and body were scrubbed to Ellen's satisfaction, and then it was time to get dressed. "Any particular gown?" Ellen asked, once all the variety of undergarments were in place.

"Since I smell of lavender," Phleg said, "why don't I put on that lavender-colored dress?"

"Very good, my lady," Ellen said. "An excellent choice."

Phleg suspected she would have said that no matter which dress Phleg had chosen, so long as it wasn't the one she had just come out of.

Dressed and combed, she followed Ellen, who, surprisingly, led her outdoors into the garden, but not to the same section where she had spied on Fred and Telmund two days ago. The two queens sat in a shady clearing, at a table that was set with fruits and a variety of breads and jellies. Fred sat there, too, though his chair wasn't pulled up to the table. He had his leg outstretched and supported by a stool.

Phleg no longer thought his curly-like-a-sheep hair looked preposterous, and she was *very* happy to see him. "Fred!" Phleg cried. Then she hastily added, ". . . Rick!"

"Princess Gabriella!" Fred held his hands out to her, which she took as a sign that she should go to him. Unexpectedly, he took both her hands, then kissed the backs of them, one after the other. "My champion," he said to her, "my guardian angel."

"Now you're just being silly," she told him, but that couldn't wipe the ridiculous grin off his face. Hers, either, she realized.

One of the queens cleared her throat.

Phleg turned and faced both queens. Which was she supposed to greet first? One was supposedly her mother, but the other was the queen of the kingdom her human family wanted to sign a treaty with, someone they wanted to impress. Besides, she felt guilty tricking Gabriella's mother. So she took a step toward Fred's mother, but in that instant saw the woman glance at the other queen. Fred's mother gave a tiny shake of her head and an almost imperceptible flick of her hand, directing Phleg to the other queen first.

"Mother," Phleg said, though she still felt reprehensible for it.

Gabriella's mother held her hands out, much as Fred had done. But once Phleg placed her hands in the queen's, the queen didn't kiss them, just clasped them as though she never wanted to let go. But then she did let go, of one of them anyway, to caress Phleg's face, all the while looking as though she couldn't get enough of her. Could she tell? Phleg wondered. Could she see there was something wrong and that Phleg was not really her daughter? Was *that* what this examination was about?

Phleg leaned in to distract her, to kiss her cheek. She was going to kiss both, the way Fred's mother had kissed both her cheeks last night, but Gabriella's mother had enough with one and threw her arms around Phleg's neck and buried her face into the space between Phleg's hair and shoulder.

"It does smell nice, doesn't it?" Phleg asked, afraid the queen was going to cry. "Ellen helped me wash it."

Gabriella's mother laughed. She dabbed at her eyes but didn't cry all out. She gave Phleg's hand one final squeeze, then let go.

Phleg turned to the other queen. She tried to remember how to curtsey, but bumped the table, so she probably got it wrong. "Um . . . hello, Queen."

She was going to just leave it at that, but the queen murmured, "Wilhelmina."

Since *her* name was supposed to be Gabriella, and there was nobody else around, Phleg deduced the woman was supplying her own name. "Hello, Queen Wilhelmina," she said, trying another curtsey, which went better than the first.

This queen held her hands out, too.

Phleg had no idea what to expect, since everyone seemed to have a different way of greeting her.

But Queen Wilhelmina just gave Phleg's hands one affectionate squeeze, then she let go. "I am so pleased to see you," she said. "Frederic has been full of stories about your bravery and your accomplishments."

"Well . . . ," Phleg said with a friendly smile in Fred's direction, ". . . don't forget your son had a fever."

Queen Wilhelmina shook her head. "I am not so much interested in the specifics as in the fact that you stayed with him while he was injured, saw to his wounds, and brought him safely back to us. You are kind, and I very much appreciate that."

Nobody had ever called Phleg kind before. "Well . . . ," she said. But she had no idea what to say next, and that eventually became obvious to everyone.

Gabriella's mother said, "Sit down. Eat. I'm afraid we've already started because the morning is so far gone."

Phleg sat down in the one remaining chair, the one closest to Fred.

He blew kisses in her direction.

Phleg looked at all the food and recalled the previous meal she'd had with Gabriella's friend Amanda. They had quarreled, and Phleg had to admit to herself that it was probably because she had done something wrong, something to arouse the other girl's suspicions. Not a clue what that could be, though. No doubt it was safest not to eat in front of the two queens and Fred . . . Well, she could probably stand on her head and recite poetry and she wouldn't arouse Fred's suspicions, but she had to be careful in front of the queens.

"I'm not so much hungry," she said. "But is there any more of that delicious milk?"

Ellen, who had been waiting silently in the background, stepped forward to pour some milk into a cup for her.

"This is just so good," Phleg said, taking a big swallow.

"What is it?" Fred asked Ellen.

"Just milk," Ellen told him, "with a little dab of honey."

Phleg, who was just turning from looking at the queens to looking at Fred, choked and coughed, spraying milk out of her mouth and onto queens, prince, and servant alike. "Honey?" she managed to gasp out between wheezing, close-to-retching coughs.

"Yes?" Ellen asked warily.

"Don't you know what honey is?" Phleg demanded. "It's bee spit!"

Ellen and the two queens looked at Phleg as though there was something wrong with *her*.

"Bee spit!" Phleg repeated, because she assumed they must not have understood. "Bees drink up nectar from flowers, then spit it out, then walk all over it, and live on it, and . . . and . . . That's disgusting."

Fred started to laugh. "Well, so it is," he admitted. "I never thought of it that way before. Gabriella, you are a wonder. Isn't she a wonder, Mother? I love the unique way she has of looking at things. I love the way she says exactly what's on her mind. Gabriella . . ." He shook his head, but not in a bad way. "Gabriella, I am so pleased I'm betrothed to you, and not to some ordinary princess."

"No," Phleg said, for he was not betrothed to her, he was betrothed to Gabriella.

A new voice thundered. Leopold's. No telling exactly when he and Gabriella's father had entered the clearing, but they were there now. "*No* is the first sensible thing the girl has said. I appreciate that she brought our son home to us—though he wouldn't have been lost in the first place but for her strange ways!" He turned to Gabriella's father. "Humphrey, she will definitely *not* be marrying my son. Much as an alliance with you would have benefited us, the betrothal is off! Wilhelmina, find Telmund. Frederic, prepare to leave. Immediately!"

We've been here before, Phleg thought. But this time there was no way Fred could run after her, even if she was able to escape the garden. Which she probably couldn't, because King Humphrey was blocking her way and eyeing her warily.

Perhaps Fred also was worried that she planned to start running, for he leaped to his feet, though a bit clumsily because of the wrappings around his leg.

But Fred didn't throw himself in Phleg's path to keep her there. Instead, he faced his father. "I love Princess Gabriella," he stated. "And I have every intention to marry her, as has been decreed by our alliance with her father."

Leopold's face turned a shade of purple Phleg had never before seen on any being, human or fairy. "How *dare* you defy me?" he sputtered. "This girl has been nothing but a bad influence on you. I say you will not marry her!"

His wife, Queen Wilhelmina, stood also. "Oh, Leopold," she said, "stop being a bully."

"I am not a bully!" Leopold roared. "I am the king. And what I say goes. And what I say is this: If King Humphrey does not agree to dissolve this proposed union between his daughter and my son, I will consider this an act of unforgivable duplicity, and I will declare war!"

King Humphrey's face was going through some purpleness of its own. "How dare you? If my daughter wants to marry your son and you stand in the way of our formal agreement and her happiness, then *I* declare war on *you*!"

~ *Chapter 10* ~

Geese and Badgers

PRINCESS GABRIELLA

Rather than sit around and worry—even though it probably would have been only Gabriella and Parf who worried, as Benlos seemed physically incapable of anything besides good cheer—the three of them decided to go outdoors and see if there were any animals who needed tending. Mumsy had already gone into the woods, putting Daisy in charge of the younger fairy children. By the sounds coming from the back rooms of the house, it seemed they were involved in some major construction or demolition work.

Benlos was kind and gentle with their patients, but didn't seem as naturally skilled at determining what ailed a creature as Parf was, unless it was obvious enough that even Gabriella could tell. On the other hand, Parf didn't ask more of his father than to calm whatever animal they were treating. Instead, he kept asking Gabriella testing questions: "What do you think?" and "What would you do?" Whatever her answer, he would invariably find fault with it. Finally Gabriella stood up from the log she was sharing with Benlos and announced that she was going to switch places with Daisy.

"Well, how do you ever expect to learn iffen you can't take anything less than all-out admiration of your wonderfulness?" Parf asked. "Is that the way they do things back at your castle? Not ask you to do much of anything, and let you give up iffen the little they expect is beyond you?"

With her hands on her hips, Gabriella mentally counted to ten. This was a strategy her diplomacy teacher had suggested for dealing with difficult foreign representatives or unruly peasants. In the past, Gabriella had never before gotten beyond *seven*. With Parf, she got to *fifty-three* and only stopped then because Parf broke her concentration by asking, "Turned to stone, have you?"

"Parf!" Benlos called.

"What?" Parf snapped. "She's exasperating! She don't even—"

He was calling *her* exasperating?

"No—*Parf*," Benlos interrupted in a this-is-important tone that caused Parf to look beyond Gabriella, and Gabriella to turn around.

Benlos stood, still holding the gosling he'd been stroking. Parf had been examining its mother, who had a foot fungus.

How strange, Gabriella thought, noting that the gosling was fading and becoming see-through. A moment later she realized that both the gosling *and* Benlos were see-through. Which must mean—

"No!" Parf shouted, getting up and shoving her out of his way.

Too late.

Benlos dissolved into a purple cloud.

The Council must have come to a decision.

Parf growled at Gabriella in frustration. "You were in the way!" he shouted. "I could've gotten to him iffen you hadn't been blocking me."

"I would have been sitting right next to him," Gabriella shot back, not shouting—not exactly, "if you hadn't been acting so pigheaded and unreasonable."

"Yeah?" Parf shouted. By then he *had* to shout, as the goose mother caught on that her goose baby was no longer there. She honked in crying out for her lost one to come back, and again in sorrow, and finally in fury. Gabriella couldn't speak goose, but the frantic mother's mood was clear. She flapped her wings, raining a flurry of feathers, and ran back and forth between where Benlos had been and where Parf was.

"Yeah?" Parf shouted again. "Well, he called for me, not you!"

Gabriella had to think. She couldn't make sense of this. "What does that have to do with anything? This isn't a competition."

Parf's jaw was set. He glared at her, but then turned his attention to trying to calm the distraught goose.

"It isn't," Gabriella protested. "You're the one who told your mother I should go to the Council hearing."

"Yeah? So what? I didn't mean for you to take over and become the favorite."

"The favorite!" Gabriella exclaimed. "Your parents have twelve children. They very obviously love you all. I'm just a changeling."

"Hmph."

Clearly his hurt feelings would not be soothed by logic.

But she couldn't help trying. "Besides," she said, "you were the one who found the tooth under the table."

"Like you wouldn't've—in another heartbeat or so? After setting everything up, talking the Council into listening, scaring Uncle Ardfogy?" He shook his head. "I knew you were trouble to begin with."

"Ha!" Gabriella said.

Parf raised an eyebrow.

"No, go on, please. Explain."

"See, that's it exactly; with your fancy la-dee-da way of talking, you're more like my father than I am."

"Don't talk to me about talking," Gabriella told Parf. "You don't talk like either of your parents—or any of your brothers or sisters."

"Oh yeah?" Parf took a step toward Gabriella, so that they were standing just about nose to nose. Well . . . in truth his nose was more aligned to her chin than any other part of her face, but he *was* standing close. "And what do you, in all your clever human princessness, think you know about that?"

Gabriella did not back away. "I think you talk the way you talk because that's what *you* choose. I think it's your way of standing out and saying, 'Nobody can tell me what to do.' I think you want to aggravate people—that's why you change everybody's names so that they all sound rude."

"Yeah?" Parf countered. "And I think you talk the way you talk because *you* think you're better than everyone else."

"I talk the way I talk to communicate with less of a chance of misunderstanding." She thought about this for a moment. "Except in your case. You *always* misunderstand. Intentionally.

195

You revel in misunderstanding. I may be a princess, but you're the King of Misunderstanding!"

Parf finally took a step back. "Maybe," he admitted. "But the big thing I just don't understand—what I really try to understand but can't—is *what is it* about my father and humans? I don't see why he's so caught up in their stories that he keeps trying to pass himself off as human, so that he can spend time among them. Nobody else's father does that. They're satisfied with the old fairy folklore. They don't need to learn more."

Gabriella tried to picture Benlos passing himself off as human. Maybe, if it was a dark night, and if he didn't sit or stand too close to anyone. And if he wore a loose cloak to hide his wings. A loose cloak with a hood to hide his silver-white hair. A loose cloak with a hood that hung low over his face to hide his purple eyes.

"Magic," she said, working it out. "That's what he uses dragons' teeth for—to disguise himself as human so he can come among us and listen to our stories."

"A bit slow, ain't you?" Parf sneered. "To just be catching on now?"

"And that's why you don't like humans in general, and me in particular."

Parf shrugged. "Well, *you've* kind of grown on me," he mumbled, turning to grab the goose so that he could finish wrapping its foot. "At first I couldn't stand how you wouldn't fight back. I thought, *How far is she going to let me push her?* But then I caught on that you could've, anytime you wanted to—you just chose not to."

Gabriella was used to diplomats and courtiers with their empty praise. But Parf's words made her blush. "And I've grown used to you," she admitted. "I admire how skilled and kind you are with the animals."

The goose began honking again, and struggling to get free of Parf's firm hold.

At which point Gabriella became aware of a honking echo. A cloud appeared by the log on which Benlos had been sitting, and then Benlos himself appeared, still holding the gosling.

He let it go as soon as he was solid enough.

Both the mother and the little one honked at each other and touched beaks; then they waddled out of the clearing, still honking. Gabriella couldn't tell if they were saying *I missed you* or *Let's get away from those three before one of us disappears again.*

"That didn't take long," Parf said.

Nodding toward the noisy baby goose, Benlos said, "Oh, the Council was quite eager to have me out of there."

"So what's the bad news?" Parf asked.

"No bad news at all. Well, not for us. They determined your uncle had lied, and so they removed him from the Council."

"That's the least they could do," Parf grumbled.

"It *was* the least they did," Benlos said. "Ardforgel and Sylvimit will be coming here later to offer a formal apology."

Parf gave a noncommittal grunt.

"And he has to pay a penalty."

Since Parf was pretending to be too uninterested to ask, Gabriella did. "To the Council?"

Benlos grinned. "To us. One dragon's tooth for each of us: me, Mumsy, each of the little ones—even Miss-mot, though hers will be held in a trust until she's a bit older—one for our changeling, and another for our daughter, whose place our changeling has taken."

Parf grunted again, although he was hard-pressed not to look pleased. "Fifteen dragons' teeth," he said. "That will be out-and-out painful for Ardfogy to give up."

Benlos held up a little pouch. Obviously, his locket could not accommodate that many teeth. "It was," he said. "And it will hurt him again every Midsummer Day and Midwinter Night when he must pay the fee again."

Even Parf could no longer keep his face sour. "Wow," he said. "Just. Wow."

Benlos opened the pouch and handed Parf a tooth. He made to hand one to Gabriella, too, but she shook her head. "Humans can't make magic," she said, "even with a dragon's tooth. So you should keep it."

"Council said it was yours," Benlos insisted. "Don't you have a wish? I could make it for you."

"Well, yes," Gabriella said. "I wish I was back home."

And, in another instant, she was.

PHLEG

The idea that these two countries could go to war because of *her* caused Phleg to do something she had never done before: She said, "I'm sorry."

And then, in another first, taking herself totally by surprise, she started to cry.

"See what you've done!" exclaimed Gabriella's mother, addressing King Leopold. "You horrid, horrid man!"

Queen Wilhelmina turned on her. "Please don't talk to my husband that way!" she snapped.

Now these two queens, who had been nothing but kind to her, were arguing—*because of her.* "I'm sorry," she repeated, her words little more than a raspy croak.

But King Humphrey heard her. "You have nothing to be sorry for!" he bellowed.

"How about spitting milk on two royal personages?" King Leopold demanded.

"She didn't mean to," said everyone else—some with more exasperation than others—Fred, his mother, Gabriella's mother, Gabriella's father, and Gabriella's servant, Ellen.

"But that was only the final straw," Leopold said. "The straw that broke the camel's back."

"Camel, my foot," Fred's mother snorted. "You're not a camel; you're a horse's rear end!" She turned to Gabriella's mother and explained, "*I* can say things like that; he's *my* husband."

While his father sputtered, Fred made his way to Phleg's side, despite the fact that he was not supposed to put any weight on his injured leg. He put his arms around her and patted her back, saying, "There, there, everything will be all right," in much the same way Phleg would have comforted a sick or hurt animal.

It was a nice feeling.

"What have you done to my daughter?" an angry voice demanded.

But it wasn't King Humphrey asking.

Phleg would have recognized this voice anywhere—even somewhere it wasn't supposed to be. It was her own true father. She lifted her wet and snotty face away from Fred's chest, just as King Humphrey, sounding pretty angry himself, demanded, "Who are these intruders? And how have they gotten into our private garden?"

And it indeed was more than just her father crowding into the grassy clearing among the hedges. It was her entire family: Parf and Mumsy and all the little ones. Even the changeling herself, Princess Gabriella.

Oops, that couldn't be good.

Nor was it good that Mumsy must have come here directly from tending animals, for under each arm she held a badger. The two animals had bite marks and scratches, evidence that Mumsy was treating wounds they had inflicted on each other in a badger dispute. Phleg's family were strict in their demand for peace among all living creatures who sought fairy help, so Phleg had no doubt that the two badgers had been behaving themselves admirably while Mumsy took care of their hurts. In normal circumstances, that peace would have continued until they made their separate ways back into the wild woods. In normal circumstances, they would not have found themselves suddenly transported via fairy magic into an entirely different environment, one filled with a variety of two-legged creatures they had never before met. Some of the two-legged creatures—fairy children and human alike—began squealing at the suddenness of their arrival.

The badgers squirmed their way out of Mumsy's grip and dropped to the ground. The two came together in a single snarling, hissing, biting, clawing ball of fur that tumbled back and forth among all those fairy and human and table legs.

If Phleg had thought there had been squealing before, that was nothing compared to the squealing that started once the badgers were loose. Her younger brothers and sisters were not used to brawling badgers, and neither—apparently—were the humans.

Fred placed himself in front of her, a gesture of protectiveness that Phleg appreciated, though considering how erratically the battling badgers were rolling about, that may not have been the most effective defense. She peeked beyond him to see what was happening.

The two queens clung to each other, screaming.

"Do something!" King Humphrey howled at Ellen, clearly deeming that badger removal was not among a king's duties.

But neither, just as clearly, did Ellen feel that was the function of a lady's maid.

King Leopold took a hurried step backward as the growling ball of badger veered suddenly in the direction of his ankles. He would have toppled over a stool, had Humphrey not caught and steadied him.

"Guards!" Humphrey bellowed. "Help!"

The only people who responded to that call for help were Princess Gabriella—the *real* Princess Gabriella—and Daisy, the oldest of Phleg's younger sisters, who had been training to tend the animals. But neither had ever separated feuding badgers before. Although the two of them kept running after the badger

201

ball, Phleg suspected that they were both earnestly hoping they would *not* catch up.

Meanwhile, Mumsy was hollering, "Quiet! Calm down, everyone! And that includes you, Sharp-Claw—and you, Scourge-of-the-Forest! Quiet! *Quiet!* QUIET!"

Unsurprisingly, her shrieking did not calm badger, fairy, or human.

Phleg saw Parf looking at her. Once she met his gaze, he said, in his irritatingly smirky tone that carried over every din, "It hasn't been three days. You lose the bet."

Her father, who had been looking appreciative of the chaos, smacked her brother on the back of the head. "No, she does not. *She* didn't come back home; *we* came here. Hello, Renphlegena."

"Hello, Daddy," Phleg said.

Fred, still standing in front of her to block the badgers, slowly turned to face her.

The wrestling badgers wrestled their way against one of the legs of the table that held the breakfast.

Phleg saw the table wobble, but before it fell she grabbed hold of the pitcher of honeyed milk. The table with all its food and dishes crashed to the ground, which finally—*finally*—startled the badgers into a moment of stillness, a brief breather in their fur-flying fury.

Phleg emptied the pitcher of milk on top of them.

Sputtering, the badgers broke off from each other, then ran off into opposite directions.

"There," Phleg said, handing the pitcher to Ellen. "That's settled."

"Isn't she remarkable!" Fred announced to everyone.

"Yes," Phleg said. "But I also am not who you think I am." It was time—it was past time—for honesty. She glanced over the crowd until she found the person she was looking for. "Princess Gabriella?"

The princess stepped into the center of the clearing, being careful not to tread on any of the broken crockery or spilled food, as she wasn't wearing shoes.

"I am so sorry," Phleg told her. "I never stopped to think how changing places with you would affect anyone besides me."

Gabriella didn't scream at her. Or slap her. Or pull her hair. All of which would have been things Phleg might have been tempted to do. Gabriella stood quietly, looking distracted.

"Say something," Phleg told her.

". . . Six," Gabriella said, ". . . seven . . ." She took a deep breath. Then inclined her head. "It has been a learning experience. Learning experiences are always of value."

Which Phleg guessed might be a princessly way of saying she forgave Phleg.

Meanwhile, the princess's parents finally looked at Gabriella— the true Gabriella. Beyond the uncombed hair and the (Phleg could tell the difference now) unprincessly clothing, something of their real daughter shone through.

The queen gasped, then held her arms wide. Gabriella ran to her.

The king cleared his throat. Looking at Phleg, he asked, "Then who, might I ask . . ."

"Phleg," Phleg said.

"Renphlegena," Mumsy and Daddy said simultaneously. Mumsy smiled at him and he went to stand by her side. "Everything's settled, then?" she asked him.

"More than settled," Daddy assured her.

"I don't understand," King Humphrey said.

"Make that two of us," King Leopold agreed.

"What's there to understand?" Fred said. "My love, who I thought was Princess Gabriella, is instead a fairy princess named Ren . . . Ren . . ."

"Phleg," Phleg repeated.

"Renphleg," Fred said.

Which was rather endearing, so Phleg didn't correct him.

"And she ain't no princess," Parf was obviously tickled to tell everyone.

Daddy said, "But she *is* the daughter of some very important fairies. Who are getting more important all the time."

Leopold was not impressed. "A fairy commoner who has been impersonating the princess whom my son was betrothed to marry." He glanced at the real princess disapprovingly, taking in her hair, face smudges, not-fit-for-a-princess dress, and bare feet. "Not that I'm convinced this one is any better. I do not believe she is acceptable at all!"

Humphrey said, "And I'm not convinced we want to be allied with *you*."

"Oh, come, Father," Gabriella said. "Obviously a lot has happened. We all need to sit down and quietly discuss this."

While the princess's parents, as well as Phleg's, as well as Queen Wilhelmina, all nodded, Leopold went, "Humph!"

His wife smacked him on the arm. When he looked at her, startled, she pretended to be vigorously brushing crumbs off his sleeve. She smiled innocently.

Fred walked away from Phleg—she had always known he would—and approached Gabriella. He took the princess's hands and looked into her eyes. "I know we were betrothed when we were children," he said, "and I came here fully intending to honor that agreement between our parents, judging that love would come once we knew each other. But in the last three days I have fallen in love with Renphleg."

Phleg's heart beat hard enough to hurt.

"Fallen in love with her?" Leopold thundered before Gabriella could answer. "You haven't even seen her real face!"

"I haven't needed to," Fred said. He let go of Gabriella's hands and returned to Phleg, taking hers.

Phleg took a deep breath. She might well lose everything, but she let the enchantment that made her look like Gabriella slip away. The lavender princess gown shifted into the form and color of the dress she'd been wearing on the day she cast the spell, the dress Mumsy had made from a sunflower. Her wings were revealed to all, as was her short, iridescent silver hair, and the fact that her height brought her to only halfway up Fred's chest.

"Oh," Fred said, sounding—could it be? Phleg wondered—sounding delighted. "Oh, Phleg, you are truly beautiful."

She needed to respond to this romantic moment. "And I don't think anymore that your hair makes you look like a sheep."

"Well, there we go!" Fred said.

"I forbid this!" If the dishes hadn't already been broken, the sheer volume of Leopold's objection would have shattered them.

"Father," Fred said. "Please forgive me for challenging you. I don't mean to defy you. But since I love . . . Phleg . . . and since I am willing to marry her—in fact *want* to marry her—in fact would be *devastated if I didn't* marry her—given all that, I don't see the problem. We can have an alliance between our kingdom and the fairy realm."

Apparently coming to the judgment that in comparison Princess Gabriella wasn't all that unacceptable after all, Leopold said, "But what about our alliance with Humphrey? Humphrey! Say something!"

Humphrey looked at his daughter.

Gabriella said, "I think that if Prince Frederic of Rosenmark and Renphlegena of the woods fairies love each other, that is an excellent start to an alliance."

Phleg tightened her hold on Fred, and he on her.

Unexpectedly—well certainly Phleg found it unexpected— Parf moved to stand by Gabriella.

"What?" Gabriella asked him.

"Nothing," he mumbled, sounding—her brother!—shy and awkward. "Just . . . you know . . . in case alliances are being made . . . It would give my father the excuse he needs to visit the human world."

Gabriella smiled at him. At Parf! "We'll see," she told him.

Meanwhile, Miss-mot had sat down on the ground and was about to scoop some of the spilled food into her mouth.

Phleg stepped forward at the same time Princess Gabriella did. They both leaned in—and clunked heads.

Of all who were there, it was King Leopold who swept the child up into his arms. "No," he said to her, firmly but not unkindly.

"You're loud," Miss-mot told him.

"Humph!" he said, but he didn't put her down.

Perfect

It is said that once there was a fairy girl and a human prince who met and fell in love, and then lived happily ever after.

It is also said that there was a human princess and a fairy boy who met, and they eventually fell in love, and then *they* lived happily ever after, too. But that one took a little more work.

About the Author

Vivian Vande Velde is the Edgar Award–winning author of *Never Trust a Dead Man*. She has also written *Heir Apparent, Dragon's Bait*, and dozens of other fantasy and mystery novels for young readers. She lives in Rochester, New York, with her husband, Jim.